"I don't know how to tell you this," Merrie said, "but we're engaged."

Dave choked. "I beg your pardon?"

Merrie didn't dare meet his eyes. "Would it help if I told you it's for a good cause?" She spilled out the whole story.

Dave murmured, "I see." He lifted his wineglass. "A toast. To our future."

Feeling dazed, Merrie clinked glasses with him. "You're really going to do it?"

"Isn't that what you wanted?" Before Merrie could respond, he brushed a kiss across her cheek.

He was going to do it! Her crazy scheme might actually work, and no harm done. Except—an old saying popped into Merrie's head. Something about jumping out of the frying pan and into the fire.

Well, it was too late to back out now.

Jacqueline Topaz

Visiting new places, meeting new people, and even making new mistakes appeal to Jacqueline Topaz, who has lived in Texas, Kentucky, Tennessee, Massachusetts, and Italy. She indulged her rampant curiosity as a reporter for the Associated Press in Los Angeles, and now covers theater for AP as a free-lancer. Although she's interviewed people such as Charlton Heston and Lynn Redgrave, she admits she's still star struck. Once when she was seated next to Bea Arthur at the theater, she hardly dared to breathe during the entire performance!

Though she now lives in southern California, Jackie never jogs or works out at a health spa; when she gets the urge to exercise, she takes two aspirin and goes to bed until it passes. She likes to spend her time reading—preferably side by side in bed with her husband, Kurt—and talking to interesting people.

Jackie draws on her daydreams for the characters and situations in her novels. Doing the research can be fun, too. To prepare for one book, she went on a national game show and ended up winning a trip to San Francisco.

Other Second Chance at Love books by
Jacqueline Topaz

SWEPT AWAY #249
RITES OF PASSION #258
LUCKY IN LOVE #297
GOLDEN GIRL #336

Dear Reader:

For March, two award-winning Second Chance at Love authors, Jan Mathews and Jacqueline Topaz, provide, respectively, a searing emotional drama and a lighthearted fairy-tale. Married to a detective herself, Jan has placed both her hero and heroine in the exciting and dangerous world of law enforcement, while Jacqueline unites a veterinarian and a wealthy executive who's not above dressing as Santa Claus or Sherlock Holmes when the situation warrants!

In *Surrender the Dawn* (#434), popular Second Chance at Love author Jan Mathews weaves a dramatic tale of love triumphant. Policewoman Laura Davis will never forget the night she was raped by a mobster. Ever since then, she's wrapped a protective shell around herself, but federal agent Kyle Patterson is determined to help Laura conquer her dark memories. He courts her with romantic sunsets on board his boat, *Sea Witch*, and reintroduces her to life's lighter moments, including a humorous episode involving a "slime monster." Fans of the hit TV series *Cagney and Lacey* and the critically acclaimed film *The Untouchables* will especially enjoy Jan's skillful combination of compelling police drama and stirring romance in *Surrender the Dawn*.

In the tradition of the classic romantic comedy film *The Philadelphia Story,* Jacqueline Topaz expertly blends lightness, laughter, and love in her fifth Second Chance at Love novel, *A Warm December* (#435). Veterinarian Merrie McGregor enjoys the simple life, and has no designs on wealthy, eligible businessman Dave Anders—but, angered by her sister's jibes at her lack of marital prospects, Merrie impulsively claims to be engaged to Dave. To Merrie's surprise, Dave's not only delighted to play along with her charade—he wants to make their betrothal a reality! And with Merrie's five-year-old niece and Dave's dog in Cupid's corner, too, Merrie's reservations must yield to Dave's persuasive charm. With an appealing cast of characters—and animals—*A Warm December* is an entertaining tour de force.

The March Berkley historical romance roster includes beloved Second Chance at Love author Jasmine Craig. We're proud to be publishing Jasmine's first longer work, *The Devil's Envoy,* set in England and the Ottoman Empire. We're also reissuing *Love, Honor, and Betray* by Elizabeth Kary, author of the Second Chance at Love novel *Portrait of a Lady* (#285) and winner of a Waldenbooks Best New Historical Romance Writer Award. For western-romance fans, we're releasing *Silver Flame* by bestselling author Susan Johnson, who received an unprecedented *six* stars from *Affaire de Coeur,* and *Savage Eden* by Cassie Edwards, winner of the 1987 *Romantic Times* Indian Series Lifetime Achievement Award. For readers who enjoy exotic settings and intrigue, we're publishing the first mass-market edition of Theresa Conway's *A Passion for Glory,* set in Revolutionary France and the American South, and reprinting the contemporary romantic-suspense classic *Dangerous Deceptions* by Arabella Seymour. Our Barbara Cartland Camfield novel of love is *Secrets of the Heart,* and our Georgette Heyer Regency reissue is *Venetia.* For mystery buffs, we're offering Edgar Award–nominee Lilian Jackson Braun's *The Cat Who Had 14 Tales,* Ngaio Marsh's *A Man Lay Dead,* and Agatha Christie's *Appointment with Death.* And, finally, we're reissuing another of Agatha Christie's romantic novels written under the pseudonym Mary Westmacott, *A Daughter's a Daughter.*

Until next month, happy reading!

Sincerely,

Hillary Cige

Hillary Cige, Editor
SECOND CHANCE AT LOVE
The Berkley Publishing Group
200 Madison Avenue
New York, NY 10016

SECOND CHANCE AT LOVE™

JACQUELINE TOPAZ
A WARM DECEMBER

BERKLEY BOOKS, NEW YORK

A WARM DECEMBER

Copyright © 1988 by Jackie Hyman

All rights reserved. No part of this publication may be repro-
duced or transmitted in any form or by any means, electronic
or mechanical, including photocopy, recording, or any information storage and retrieval system, without permission in
writing from the publisher.

Requests for permission to make copies of any part of the
work should be mailed to: Permissions, Second Chance at
Love, The Berkley Publishing Group, 200 Madison Avenue,
New York, NY 10016.

First edition published March 1988

ISBN: 0-425-10683-7

"Second Chance at Love" and the butterfly emblem are trade-
marks belonging to Jove Publications, Inc. The name "BERK-
LEY" and the "B" logo are trademarks belonging to Berkley
Publishing Corporation.

Second Chance at Love books are published by
The Berkley Publishing Group
200 Madison Avenue, New York, NY 10016

Printed in the United States of America

10 9 8 7 6 5 4 3 2 1

For Virginia and Joe

CHAPTER
One

WEARY FROM A LONG Saturday—of which the highlight had been extracting birdshot from the rump of an over-eager cocker spaniel—Meredith McGregor, D.V.M., was shrugging off her white coat when an angry male voice from the front office broke into her thoughts.

"What do you mean, you closed ten minutes ago? It's only five after six!"

"All right, we closed *five* minutes ago." Patience strained against irritation in the voice of Alida Reese, who doubled as a receptionist and animal technician.

"I was held up in traffic," he snapped, as if Alida were somehow to blame. "You'd think they could put an interstate highway through Nashville without tearing up half the city. Well, I'm here, and I've come to collect my dog."

"I'll see what I can do." Tight-lipped, Alida appeared in the hallway of the old house that had been remodeled into a veterinary clinic long ago. "Dr. McGregor? Can you release"—she checked the dog's name on a card in her hand and pronounced it sarcastically—"Champion Reeves Philton Conqueror?"

Merrie groaned inwardly. She'd been looking forward to kicking off her shoes and relaxing over a hot meal, the sooner the better. Still, she didn't like leaving an animal in the center over a Sunday if it wasn't essen-

1

tial. "Didn't Dr. Brown leave instructions? It must be his patient."

"Oh." Alida consulted the card. "Yes. It's okay." The phone rang. "Darn! We're shorthanded—Jenny went home sick." She raced out of sight around the corner.

Champion Reeves Philton Conqueror. Merrie immediately pictured a clipped, high-strung poodle and an owner to match. She would let Alida handle this one.

Merrie had other things to think about. Like Christmas coming up on Friday. And a waif of a little girl who needed her help. And—

"Miss?" The masculine voice made her turn sharply. "I'm Dave Anders, and I'd like my dog, please. Your friend seems to be tied up on the phone."

The man standing in the doorway fixed her with steely gray eyes, obviously accustomed to commanding obedience. From his height and the way his tailored coat fit over broad shoulders, she guessed he would intimidate most women. But most women weren't five feet nine and fully capable of administering antibiotics to a horse.

Without her coat, Merrie realized, he must have mistaken her for one of the technicians. "I'm sure Alida will be finished in a minute."

"Look, I'm in a hurry. Do you mind?"

Yes, she did mind, but it would probably be easier to release Champion Reeves Philton Conqueror to his owner than to stand here arguing about it.

"All right. This way." She led him into a room lined with steel cages, mostly empty now. From nearby came the high-pitched gabbling of Britches, a spider monkey who had accidentally slashed his hand when he grabbed his mistress's cooking knife. Merrie clucked to the animal as she passed, and reminded herself to check that Britches had enough food and water. Jenny, the teenager who worked here on Saturdays, had been exercising Britches just before she went home sick, and might have forgotten something.

An excited bark came from a large cage at the end, and Merrie saw that it was not a poodle but a doe-eyed collie, his feathery tail fluttering with excitement.

"Hey, Buster." Dave Anders dropped to one knee after a quick glance at the linoleum to make sure his crisp wool pants wouldn't be spoiled.

"Buster?" Merrie couldn't help being amused. "You call Champion Reeves Philton Conqueror just plain Buster?"

The man went right on talking to his dog as if he hadn't heard. "Did they take good care of you? Poor fellow, we were worried about that lump, weren't we? But it wasn't anything serious, after all." Finally, he noticed Merrie again. "Would you please let him out? I haven't got time to—"

The rattle of metal behind her made Merrie pivot just as the door to Britches's cage swung open. Hurrying toward it, she fumed silently at Jenny. Even illness was no excuse for not making sure a cage was latched properly. Monkeys were notorious escape artists.

Fast as she was, she wasn't quick enough. The tiny, long-armed creature slipped through the opening with a triumphant shriek and shimmied across the face of the cages, the bowed bending of his arms and legs emphasizing his resemblance to a spider.

"Alida!" Merrie could see she was going to need help with this one. Monkeys were not only hard to catch, they could make a mess if they began throwing bottles of medication, and they could inflict some nasty bites.

Dave Anders straightened up, his mouth twisting in annoyance. "I had no idea things had gotten so slipshod around here. Old Dr. Brown would never have allowed it."

This was no time to argue. "Just step out of the room." Merrie felt a twinge of pleasure when her authoritative tone brought a look of surprise. "Out!"

"Don't be ridiculous." To her dismay, he reached for the monkey. Visions of injuries and lawsuits danced through her brain.

"Stop it right now, Mr. Anders! I don't know what you're used to, but I'm in charge around here."

Too late. Man and monkey met, and monkey conquered—not with a bite, but by leaping onto the shoulder of Dave Anders's expensive coat, executing a caper across his stylishly trimmed brown hair, and using his arrogant head as a launchpad from which to attack a shelf full of equipment.

"Dammit! See what you've done?" Merrie pushed past the man and snatched up a blanket from the shelf. Chittering happily, Britches was hurling supplies onto the floor as she approached. But as Merrie poised to envelop him with the blanket, the monkey leaped again and scampered straight toward the door that led to the rest of the building.

Diving after him, Merrie flung the blanket over the reddish-brown form and stamped on two sides of the cloth to halt the little creature. A pair of Italian leather shoes snapped down on the other corners, and Britches was trapped.

"Thank goodness." Only then did Merrie realize that Dave Anders was standing almost toe-to-toe with her, his face inches from hers. The scent of his after-shave lotion tingled across her senses. "You . . . Thanks . . . I . . ."

Without warning, his mouth closed over hers, and his strong hands caressed her shoulders. The touch was gentle, almost playful. Dazed, Merrie took a moment before she drew back.

"Sorry." A lazy grin told her Dave wasn't sorry at all. "I guess you bring out my jungle instincts."

As if on cue, Britches hissed angrily from below and struggled against his blanket covering. "Alida!" Merrie called again, and this time the assistant came running. Donning protective gloves, Alida soon had the monkey back in the cage, and Champion Reeves Philton Conqueror—alias Buster—out of his.

"I'm really sorry, Dr. McGregor," Alida said as she replenished the monkey's food and water and headed back to the front office. "I should have double-checked everything after Jenny left."

"Just go ahead and close up for the day," Merrie called after her. "And thanks for your help with Britches."

Dave, ruffling his collie's fur affectionately, studied Merrie with interest. "So you're a vet. I've never kissed a vet before."

Heat stung Merrie's cheeks. "I hope you enjoyed yourself, Mr. Anders."

"Oh, I did. And so did you." Teasing gray eyes stared into her hazel ones. "If I didn't have a commitment for tonight, I'd suggest we explore this interesting subject further."

"I think we've explored it quite far enough." She tried to regain a measure of composure. "And it so happens I also have a commitment for tonight, for which you've made me late." She saw no reason to add that the commitment was to have dinner with her grandmother, who lived next door to her.

He straightened, snapping a leash to Buster's collar. "As I see it, you owe me something."

"I beg your pardon?"

"If it weren't for me, this place would have been empty when the monkey got out. He'd have had a fine time going AWOL overnight, wouldn't you say?"

The very idea sent shudders down Merrie's spine. "I'll concede that the timing was fortunate, but I believe you've been amply rewarded."

"I'm not trying to get out of paying my bill, you know." He looked amused at the notion. "Perhaps we could make it another night. I'm tied up through Wednesday—"

"So am I," Merrie said, although what she planned to be busy with was wrapping gifts. "And also on Thursday night, which happens to be Christmas Eve. So—"

"Too bad." Dave Anders clicked his tongue at Buster, who panted appreciatively. "I happen to be free Christmas Eve. Sure you couldn't change things around?"

The nerve of the man! "Absolutely sure." Merrie moved decisively toward the door. "I believe Alida would like to get home, if you'd care to settle your account."

"My pleasure." Dave followed her out the door. "Merry Christmas, Dr. McGregor."

"Merry Christmas."

As she changed from her rubber-soled work shoes into a pair of low-cut boots, Merrie was embarrassed to discover that her lips were still tingling. How could she have stood there as stunned as a schoolgirl? Dave Anders might be handsome, but she wasn't impressed.

Well, all right, she *was* impressed, she admitted silently as she slipped on her fake-fur coat. And he was just the sort of man her mother would approve of: rich and good-looking. Georgia Hixton McGregor Aston Lemoins, better known as Gigi Lemoins since her third marriage two years ago, had approved of a few too many men, in her daughter's opinion.

Locking the back door of the clinic behind her, Merrie set off through the crisp winter evening to her house two blocks away. There was a poignant sadness to Nashville at this time of year, the trees bare and black against the dark sky, the air smelling faintly of old leaves and fireplaces. She hoped it would snow. Steffie deserved a special Christmas.

Merrie had spent most of the previous evening buying toys for the five-year-old: a giant Big Bird, a coloring book with the largest box of crayons in existence, and a Dr. Seuss book. No need to buy clothes. If there was one thing Steffie would have, it was lots of expensive clothes.

The last thing Merrie had expected from her flighty sister Lizabeth, a New York model who took after their mother when it came to evaluating men, was for her to adopt a little girl. At thirty-one, two years older than Merrie, Lizabeth had never been interested in children, not even during her brief marriage.

Then recently, although she looked no older than she ever had, Lizabeth had begun talking about the biological clock. No doubt some of her jet-set friends were having babies, and suddenly Lizabeth wanted one, too. Not at the diaper stage, of course; instead, she'd adopted a five-year-old this fall.

Merrie had gone to New York for Thanksgiving—Lizabeth had the dinner catered—and fell in love with shy little Steffie. She'd been dismayed to learn that the child was spending most of her time with one hired nurse after another. And then, this past week, Lizabeth had announced she simply couldn't resist an invitation to go skiing in Switzerland over Christmas and visit their mother in the south of France.

So Steffie was coming to Nashville. One of Lizabeth's friends was keeping the little girl for a few days and then would fly down and drop her off Thursday en route to Florida. Merrie muttered angrily to herself, at the thought of Steffie being shuffled here and there as if the child had no feelings.

It was up to Merrie, with the aid of Grandma Netta, to make sure Steffie had the best Christmas ever. She wished she could think of some way to make the holiday really special, some surprise that Steffie would remember happily after she went back to New York.

Anger carried Merrie rapidly home. She was due at Netta's, but first she stopped off in her own two-story brick house to feed her pets.

As always, a sense of peace flowed through her as she stepped through the front hall into the living room. She'd purposely decorated it with the softest pieces she could find—a big fluffy rug, low comfortable couches, shaggy wall hangings. By the window stood the Christmas tree Merrie had wrestled home Friday evening with the help of her partner, Bill Brown, and his wife, Sue. Hung with candy canes and tiny wooden soldiers, the old-fashioned tree spread its branches above Merrie's collection of stuffed animals. The small perky rabbits, the inquisitive bears, and the droopy-antlered moose she'd brought back from a vacation in Canada made the room come alive.

A movement to her right caught Merrie's attention. It was followed by a plaintive meow.

"Okay, Homebody." She went into the kitchen to open the cat food and nearly tripped over Snoozer, who was lying by the stove soaking up the warmth from the pilot light. "Where's Wanderer?"

As if on cue, a black nose poked through the cat door from the back porch, followed by the splotchy black-

and-white form of Wanderer. Merrie would have sworn that Wanderer had a Dalmatian somewhere in his background, if he hadn't been a cat.

They needed no urging to gather around the food bowl and dig in. Only Snoozer hung back, reluctant to give up his prime spot. "Suit yourself." Merrie ran a hand over his thick orange fur. "I'm going to Netta's for dinner."

She'd coveted this house ever since she lived next door as a teenager, imagining herself moving in here someday with a husband and children of her own. Well, that part hadn't come true yet, but a least she'd been able to afford the mortgage payments when the house finally came up for sale four years ago, just after she and Bill took over his father's old veterinary clinic.

Inexplicably, Merrie found herself wondering what kind of house Dave Anders lived in. Probably a condominium, although that wouldn't leave much room for Buster to romp in.

She wished she hadn't given in to his kiss. He was right, she *had* enjoyed it. If only Merrie could respond that way to one of the men she dated from time to time. At least they fit in with her casual lifestyle. Somehow she couldn't picture Dave popping over to help her cook meat loaf or plant tomatoes in the spring or enjoy a Saturday night at the Grand Ole Opry.

After running upstairs to feed the guinea pigs, Munchkin and Grumpus, Merrie bounced over to Grandma Netta's house. She could smell the gingerbread as she crossed the yard.

Letting herself in by the kitchen door, Merrie inhaled deeply. "Smells wonderful."

Her grandmother turned away from the stove. Salt-and-pepper hair framed a handsome high-browed face, remarkably unlined at seventy-six. Merrie could still see traces of the beauty her grandmother had been as a young woman. "About time you got here. Emergency?"

"Not exactly." Merrie gave her a brief description of the monkey's escape. "I did promise to check on things tomorrow, though. After all, I'm taking off early on Thursday to pick up Steffie." Fortunately, since the Nashville Pet Emergency Center was open overnight and on weekends to take urgent cases, she and Bill didn't have to worry about being called out late at night the way Bill's father had before he retired.

Without being asked, Merrie set the kitchen table and helped her grandmother serve up the beef stew and gingerbread. It tasted heavenly.

"Say." Netta regarded her over a spoonful of stew. "Aren't you going to that Christmas party tomorrow? The one for the kids?"

Merrie nodded. She'd promised to bring the guinea pigs to a party for a group of foster children at a recreational center. "I'll only have to be at the clinic for half an hour. Alida will take care of the feedings."

Her grandmother poured herself a second cup of hot tea. "I'm not sure I shouldn't cancel out for Christmas Eve. I ought to be here with you and Steffie."

Each year, Netta and a group of friends sang carols at convalescent homes. "Don't be silly. You can't let your friends down. We'll see you Christmas morning."

They talked over some ideas for surprising Steffie but failed to come up with anything exciting. Finally, a comfortable silence fell between them, an easy familiarity bred of years spent in each other's company. It was with Netta that fourteen-year-old Merrie had stayed when her mother married for the second time and moved away from Nashville, after years of flitting in and out of her daughters' lives while Netta held down the fort.

Lizabeth, then sixteen, had been eager to move to Manhattan with her mother, but Merrie had stayed right here until she finished high school. Then she'd joined her mother and sister for a year in New York, a year that almost resulted in a disastrous marriage.

Now, secure in her grandmother's kitchen, Merrie's traitorous thoughts returned to Dave Anders. He obviously didn't place much value on holiday celebrations, the way he'd tried to make a date with her for Christmas Eve. He ought to be home with his family, if he had one.

Grandma Netta had lived in Nashville most of her life. Maybe she knew something about him.

Hoping her grandmother wouldn't notice the catch in her voice, Merrie said, "By the way, that man who helped me with the monkey was named Dave Anders. You don't happen to know him, do you?"

Netta wasn't fooled for an instant by Merrie's pretended casualness. "Piqued your interest, did he?"

"Netta! It's just idle curiosity."

"Hah." Her gandmother brought out a bottle of sherry and poured them each a splash in sparkling crystal glasses. "Nothing about Dave Anders is idle. Or you either, my girl."

"So you do know him." Merrie sipped the rich liquid. The warmth of the large kitchen was making her sleepy.

"Know *of* him, more like." Netta regarded her glass thoughtfully. "And his parents. Father's dead now. Ever heard of Anders Enterprises?"

Merrie had a sinking feeling. "You mean that big building out on Thompson Lane? Don't they make heavy equipment or something like that?"

"They make something like just about everything," her grandmother said. "Gotten into computers these last few years, so I read in the paper. Rich enough to turn even your mother's head, if she'd been lucky enough to meet 'em."

Or Lizabeth's, Merrie thought with a pang. Yes, with his tailored suit and wealthy background, Dave Anders would suit Merrie's sister perfectly. Except that the dog would have to go. Lizabeth didn't like animals.

"But Georgia—I just can't call my daughter Gigi, even if she *is* married to a Frenchman—she's just never been in the same league as Sarah Anders," Netta went on. "Guess they might have known each other at school; they both went to Harpeth Hall. But Sarah—well, she's old Nashville, a real society lady. I wouldn't be surprised if she still wears white gloves and a hat whenever she goes out. I'll bet she'd like to see that son of hers married off to some debutante at the Belle Meade Country Club."

"Well, he's got a nice dog," Merrie said.

Her grandmother laughed and pushed her chair back from the table. "That's my girl! I never met a more down-to-earth child than you were, Merrie, and heaven knows how you got that way, raised from pillar to post as you were."

"I got it from you." Merrie smiled fondly. "And he *does* own a nice dog, even if it has a name as long as your arm." She began clearing the dishes away before Netta could rise. "You cooked; now you rest."

"Never thought I'd say it, but you could do a lot worse than Dave Anders."

The remark was so unexpected that Merrie wasn't sure she'd heard correctly. "I wasn't planning to marry the man! I just met him, and I'll probably never see him again." The words rang hollowly through her mind. That lazy grin, that commanding presence of his...

Dave Anders wasn't going to be easy to forget, even after one encounter.

"I'm not the type to push, " Netta said. "And I'm in no hurry to have a great-grandchild next door. But he's got a mind of his own, that fella, and I respect him for it. Gets his name in the paper for one cause or another all the time."

"Rich people are always making donations. For the tax write-off." Years of listening to her mother's friends had taught Merrie a certain cynicism. "Well, I'm bushed. Thanks for a fabulous dinner, as usual, Netta."

She kissed her grandmother good night and went next door. Home to her guinea pigs and her cats.

The house felt larger than usual and a little bit lonely. Waiting for Steffie, Merrie told herself firmly. And someday for a man, too, of course. But not one like Dave Anders, who lived in the glitzy, brittle world coveted by her mother and sister.

Nevertheless, she sat for a long time staring at the winking light of the Christmas tree, her heart swelling with a bittersweet mixture of nostalgia and yearning.

CHAPTER
Two

MERRIE WAS AWAKENED Sunday morning by the thump of Homebody landing on her stomach. After sleepily stroking the cat and scratching her behind the ears, she arose with a yawn and went downstairs to read the comics in *The Tennessean* and linger over coffee and toast.

Doughnuts. That was what she really wanted. Merrie didn't have too many memories of her father, a country singer who'd been killed in a plane crash when she was seven, but she did remember that he used to go out for doughnuts on Sunday mornings and bring home a box still hot from the bakery oven.

A glance at her watch showed that she'd dallied too long. Merrie fed the cats, put Munchkin and Grumpus in their traveling cage, and hurried out to her beat-up station wagon.

She parked in front of the Brown Animal Center, whose name had given rise to more than a few jokes. It had been established some thirty years ago by Bill's father and then handed down to him. He'd asked Merrie, an old high school friend and a classmate from the University of Georgia, to join him in the practice, and she'd been delighted.

Carrying the guinea pigs inside and leaving them in her office, Merrie inhaled the scent of dog and antiseptic that had seeped into the floors of the old house. No matter how thoroughly the place was cleaned, it would smell this way forever.

Alida had already finished feeding and exercising the animals. With her assistance, Merrie administered medications and checked wounds. Fortunately, there were no serious problems. Even Britches seemed more or less subdued today, although Merrie thought she saw a triumphant gleam in his small eyes.

After washing up, she carried the rodents back to her car and headed for the recreational center. She was looking forward to helping bring the holiday spirit to the children, and in the process, to educating them a little about animals and their needs.

It was only a quarter after twelve as she neared her destination, and the party didn't start until one o'clock. Checking the animals hadn't taken as long as she'd expected. The sight of a doughnut shop was all she needed to make up her mind to stop.

Again, she took the guinea pigs inside with her, since they were sensitive to cold. In their cage, they shouldn't bother the other diners.

Actually, the place was nearly empty. One old man sat at the counter reading a newspaper, seemingly indifferent to the wonderful fragrances filling the air, and a woman and a small boy were just departing with their sack of goodies.

Setting the cage in a booth, Merrie went over to inspect the fresh-baked doughnuts. The air was so thick with bakery smells that she could almost taste the chocolate and maple icing, the brightly colored sprinkles, the spongy cake doughnuts and the sugary frosted ones.

It was hard to narrow down her choices, but finally Merrie selected three doughnuts and ordered a cup of coffee. Sitting down, she closed her eyes, savoring the treat.

She scarcely noticed the door opening except for the draft of cold air across her cheeks. Finishing the first doughnut, Merrie noted vaguely that a man was standing with his back to her at the counter.

As she bit into the second pastry—chocolate glazed, her favorite—a figure loomed over her.

"Mind if I join you? All the other seats seem to be taken."

Merrie coughed and stared up into the teasing gray eyes of Dave Anders. For a moment, to her embarrassment, she couldn't think of anything to say. Perhaps it was the way he towered over her, or the fact that she wasn't wearing her authoritative Dr. McGregor persona, which made him seem larger than life today. A dark blue cashmere sweater emphasized his ruddy complexion and broad chest, and the memory of his kiss tingled across her lips.

To her relief, Dave didn't seem to notice her awkwardness as he swung into the seat across from her and set his coffee and doughnuts on the table. "Hi, there," he said to the guinea pigs. "Nice of the doc to take you on an outing."

"You're lucky it isn't the day I bring my ocelot." Somehow talking about animals loosened Merrie's tongue. "How's Buster?"

"Happy to be home." Dave dug into a cream-filled doughnut as if consuming it were a serious business.

Merrie wondered idly what brought him to this part of town. It certainly wasn't the swankiest section. There were a lot of pieces to the puzzle that was Dave Anders, she was beginning to realize, but this was one puzzle she didn't intend to solve. Still, it felt uncomfortable, sitting here in silence. "Do you have a lot of dogs?" she asked, to make conversation.

"Do you always talk about animals?"

The question surprised her. "What's wrong with that?"

He didn't answer the question directly. "You know, I would never have picked you out as a veterinarian."

Merrie bristled. "Why not? I'm tall enough to handle myself just fine, and besides, being a vet isn't a matter of brute strength."

"That's not what I meant." There was something keenly personal in the way he regarded her. "I suppose the short haircut is practical, but that reddish-blond color is downright provocative, and I'll bet it's natural."

"Of course it's—"

"And I can't quite figure out the color of your eyes. Yesterday I thought they were brown, but today I could swear they're green."

His words soothed across Merrie's skin like fingertips, probing gently, tantalizing her nerve endings. "Hazel." Her voice came out in a whisper.

"I know women who would kill for those cheekbones. But you'd have been wasted as a model." He reached out and flicked a sugar crystal from her lip. "Too intelligent. I'd have pegged you as an attorney. Lethal in the courtroom, and just as devastating to a man alone with you."

The squeal of a guinea pig snapped Merrie out of her daze. "Hey. I've got to go." She stuffed her remaining doughnut ungraciously into her mouth, and then wondered why she was acting like such a nerd. *"Mumble mumble kids mumble mumble hurry mumble bye."* She narrowly avoided jamming the cage in the door on her way out.

As she started the car, Merrie fumed inwardly. What on earth had gotten into her? She'd flirted with men before, including some very handsome ones, without tripping over her own tongue. And while she may have chosen to work in a down-to-earth milieu, she'd wasted a good portion of her eighteenth year in New York, gliding in and out of restaurants and penthouses with her mother and Lizabeth. She was hardly a country bumpkin.

Drat Dave Anders anyway. She simply hadn't been prepared for his seductive manner, not in a doughnut shop on a Sunday morning.

Merrie pulled into the parking lot of the nearby recreational center and unloaded Munchkin and Grumpus, who were scrabbling about in their cramped cage. The business of finding the hostess and staking out a suitable corner of the room provided a welcome distraction.

Although the party wouldn't start for another ten minutes, children were already wandering in. Volunteers were almost finished setting out cookies and cupcakes, and hanging candy canes on a large, slightly lopsided Christmas tree.

A clown warmed up with some cartwheels as Merrie took the guinea pigs out and knelt on the floor to show them to the early arrivals. The youngsters squeezed around, full of delight and questions, eager to hold the furry creatures.

Merrie asked the children about their own pets, slipping in bits of information about how to care for the animals in cold weather. She was so absorbed in her task that she didn't notice the other goings-on until one of the children cried, "It's Santa!"

A well-stuffed figure in a red-and-white suit filled the doorway, his white beard jiggling as he *ho-ho-hoed*. Over his shoulder was slung a bag packed with gifts, enough to go around among the thirty or forty children who now filled the room.

"Who's been good all the time?" bellowed Santa.

"Me!" "I have!" answered a few children.

"And who's been good most of the time?"

"Here, Santa!" "That's me!" The room filled with eager responses.

"And who's tried real, real hard but only managed to be good once in a while?"

"You're lookin' for me, Santa!" a cocky little boy with buck teeth piped up.

"Do you promise to do better next year?" The big, rotund elf fixed the child with a baleful eye.

"I do, honest!"

"Well, I've got presents for all of you, then!"

As high-pitched voices shouted with glee, Merrie was struck by a wonderful idea. Suppose Santa came to call on Steffie!

What child wouldn't be thrilled by a personal visit from Saint Nick? She wouldn't mind paying the Santa; it would be worth it.

She watched the red-suited man as he gathered the children around him, joking and handing out dolls and teddy bears, books and games. He was perfect for the job, jolly and obviously enjoying himself.

"Who is that?" Merrie asked one of the volunteers. "Is he connected with the center?"

"I don't know. Better ask the hostess."

But the large woman who'd organized the party was on the far side of the room, busy with the kids. Well, Merrie supposed there were services she could call to rent a Santa—but they were probably all booked up by now. If this fellow was a volunteer, though, he might be willing to spare a few minutes from his Christmas Eve to help her out.

So she waited until the last present had been distributed and the last cookie crumbled into a little mouth. The guinea pigs were getting cranky from all the handling, so she tucked them back into their cage, where they nestled into sleep. And she set out to talk to Santa Claus.

He was shooing a last devoted toddler out the door as Merrie approached. "Excuse me."

"Ho ho ho!" The man reached into his pack and handed her a shiny blue yo-yo.

Merrie tried to give it back. "I wondered if—"

"And have you been a good girl this year?" he bellowed. It was impossible to tell how old he was or even what he really looked like, the way he kept winking at people across the room.

She smiled. "Most of the time."

"Well, shame on you!" He took the yo-yo back.

"I wondered if you could help me out."

"Anything, missy! Just name the time and place!" He pressed the yo-yo on one of the volunteers.

She explained briefly about Steffie and gave the man her address. "About eight o'clock? I'd be happy to pay you."

"Not necessary!" Santa waved her away. "Ho ho ho! Happy to do it!"

Walking back to her guinea pigs, Merrie felt a twinge of uneasiness. She didn't even know the man's name, and she couldn't have identified him to save her life. Yet she'd just given him her address.

Well, if you couldn't trust Santa Claus, whom *could* you trust?

Still, she looked around for the hostess, but the woman had disappeared. After waiting a few minutes, Merrie collected her guinea pigs and went out to the car.

She spotted him half a parking lot away—Santa, climbing into a gray Mercedes. Merrie waved, hoping to catch his attention. At least she could ask his name and phone number, in case she needed to reach him for some reason. But he didn't see her, and his car pulled toward the exit from the lot.

Feeling more and more uncomfortable about her impulsive behavior, Merrie started up her station wagon. Since they seemed to be going in the same direction anyway, she decided to follow the car. At least she'd have an idea where the guy lived.

Just about a mile from the center, the Mercedes slowed. Merrie, trailing some distance behind, didn't see the reason at first, and then she noticed four boys on the sidewalk.

Three of them appeared to be arguing with a fourth, who was smaller but clearly standing up for himself. As she watched, one of the bigger boys gave the outsider a shove.

At a bellow from the curb, the boys jerked around to see a towering Santa Claus striding toward them. Mouths agape, they quailed before a tirade that was audible even to Merrie. "And what have we here? Is this the Christmas spirit? I don't suppose you young men expect any toys after acting this way, now do you?"

Shamefaced, the three larger boys shook their heads in misery. The fourth watched with joy written plain across his face. Merrie's eyes stung. She'd never seen a youngster's fantasy come to life right in front of him before.

"Now, what's this all about?" Santa listened carefully as the boys explained their dispute in voices too high-pitched to carry to where Merrie's station wagon waited down the block, half-hidden behind some parked cars. "Well, I don't think that was worth all that fighting, do you?"

"No, Santa!" The largest of the boys stared up at him tearfully. "You ain't really going to pass us by this year, are you?"

"Are you all going to be friends now?"

"You bet, Santa!"

With a nod, the pudgy red figure strode to the trunk of the car and pulled out some remaining gifts. Three small ones were distributed to the bigger boys, and the largest gift went to their new pal. "You remember to be good this year, or you'll be hearing from me!"

With a wave, the Santa drove away from the curb. Chuckling, Merrie started up her car again, her concerns forgotten. Whoever this man was, he made a perfect Santa, and Steffie was going to love him.

At the next corner, the Mercedes stopped for a red light. From behind, Merrie could see the man try to scratch his head, then pull off the tasseled cap, revealing a disordered shock of brown hair. A moment later, he stripped off the white beard as well.

The light switched to green and the Mercedes made a left turn. As it did, Merrie caught a glimpse of the man in the Santa suit.

It was Dave Anders.

A lot of things made sense all at once. His presence in the doughnut shop in this unlikely part of town. The generous gifts. The Mercedes. Grandma Netta had been right: He had a mind of his own, and a concern for good causes.

Merrie was still grinning to herself over the incident with the four boys as she headed for home. It wasn't until she turned onto her block that it struck her.

Dave Anders was going to spend Christmas Eve with her and Steffie.

CHAPTER
Three

THE WEEK PASSED SLOWLY. Although quite a few animals were brought into the clinic for holiday-related injuries ranging from eating the ornaments to venturing too close to the fireplace, few people bothered with routine vaccinations and neuterings. And it didn't take long to wrap gifts for Steffie and Netta; those for Lizabeth and Gigi had been mailed long ago.

Because she loved the bustle of the season and the smells of pine and cinnamon, Merrie spent several evenings wandering through shopping malls. She would treat herself to a cookie or a cup of hot chocolate, linger in a toy store picking out stocking stuffers, or just relax on a bench to watch the parents frantically buying last-minute gifts for their children.

Unaccountably, she found herself pausing in the men's section of Cain-Sloan department store, sniffing at cologne and wondering what Dave Anders would like for Christmas. Of course, he probably didn't really need anything, but Santa deserved a reward for all his hard work.

She hadn't shopped for a man in more than ten years, apart from token gifts for Bill and other platonic friends. Ten years ago ... or was it eleven? Strange that she couldn't quite remember what had seemed, at the time, like the most important relationship of her life.

Inhaling the leather of a handcrafted wallet reminded

Merrie of Franco. Franco Meroni. Her mother had introduced him as an exciting new Italian designer. And he *had* been exciting in a way; certainly he was more sophisticated than the boys Merrie had dated in high school. At eighteen, she'd been eager to please, in love with the idea of love. And Franco had admired her fresh young looks, had taken her everywhere in New York, displaying her—she later realized—as a kind of showcase lover. Dear heaven, she'd nearly married the man!

It was sheer good luck that they'd taken the weekend trip to New England that spring, and seen the inn with the sign that read NO CHILDREN, NO PETS. Franco had stopped the car. "We'll stay here tonight," he'd said. "There is my motto."

"I'm not surprised," Merrie had answered. "After all, you're single."

"No, no." He clucked at her condescendingly. "That is the way life should be. Children and pets are for peasants."

His words had brought Merrie face to face with herself. It hadn't taken more than a few days of hard thinking to realize that she didn't belong in Franco's world, or in her mother's. And she'd begun thinking about a career, something that would involve both children and pets . . .

Well. It was amazing what the smell of leather could bring back.

Looking over the gifts, Merrie decided she didn't want to buy Dave a tie or a handkerchief or a shaving kit. So, even though she knew it was foolish, she went back to a toy store and bought a stuffed collie that looked a little like Buster. If Dave didn't want it, he must have some young relative who would enjoy it.

Returning home, Merrie wrapped the collie, put it out of sight, and turned her thoughts to the arrival of her newly acquired niece. If only it would snow. . .

And on Thursday it did. By the time Steffie's plane landed at Nashville Airport that afternoon, thick white clouds were billowing out of the sky. Merrie had been afraid the flight would be rerouted, but although the snowfall was heavy, not much had accumulated on the ground yet.

She hugged herself with nervous excitement as she waited in the lounge, peering through the debarking passengers for a glimpse of the wistful small girl. There hadn't been much time to get to know each other at Thanksgiving, but Steffie had shared Merrie's lively interest in animals and had brightened at the prospect of someday coming to Nashville and meeting the cats and guinea pigs.

Still, you never knew with children, especially when they'd had such a difficult life. Steffie might be all tears and temper, or sullen and silent. But Merrie knew that even if she couldn't reach the girl, Homebody or Snoozer or Wanderer would. And there was always Grandma Netta and her gingerbread to win through to a walled-off heart.

Suddenly, Merrie spotted a small red coat bobbing alongside a tall woman with a pinched-in nose and designer makeup. Lizabeth's Florida-bound friend, no doubt.

"Over here!" Merrie stepped forward.

"Well, thank goodness. I've got a connection in half an hour." The woman shook her hand free from Steffie's. "You must be Meredith? Well, here's her luggage stubs. There are two pieces; they're Gucci, you can't miss them."

"Thank you for taking care of her." Merrie could see from the child's withdrawn expression that the last few days hadn't been pleasant ones. Anger surged up in

Merrie at Lizabeth's carelessness. Not that Lizabeth would ever be intentionally cruel, but she was basically self-absorbed, and probably always would be.

"Well, she wasn't much trouble. She doesn't even eat much." The woman glanced at her diamond-encrusted watch. "I've got to go."

"Have a good time." Somehow it didn't seem appropriate to wish this woman a Merry Christmas. It was with relief that Merrie watched her click away through the crowd. "Hi." She knelt and faced the little girl. "Do you remember me?"

"Yes. You're Aunt Merrie." Steffie shook forward a haze of dark hair, shielding herself from the world.

"Do you remember that I promised someday you'd get to meet my cats and my guinea pigs?"

"I remember." But there was no smile, just a solemn expression that looked out of place on one so young.

"Well, we'd better get your luggage so we can go home." Merrie hoped her house really would feel like home to Steffie.

As they took the escalator down to the baggage area, Steffie clung to Merrie's hand and stared straight ahead, as if she were afraid to take too much interest in her surroundings, afraid that anything she cared about would soon be snatched away.

Maybe I'm reading too much into this, Merrie thought, but she doubted it.

They collected the luggage and stepped out into a whitening world. "It's really coming down," Merrie observed. "Was it snowing in New York?"

"A little," Steffie said. "Do you have a Christmas tree?"

"We certainly do." Merrie led her on the crosswalk to the parking lot and headed for her station wagon.

"Is it a real tree? Does it smell nice?"

"It smells wonderful." Merrie loaded the suitcases into the back and buckled Steffie into her seat. "And we're going to bake cookies and have a wonderful surprise tonight." Then a dismaying thought struck her. "Unless the snow's too heavy. Then, well, maybe we'll have a surprise tomorrow instead."

The possibility that Dave might not be able to make it tonight if the roads were blocked hadn't occurred to her until now. Certainly it would be unfortunate, but that didn't explain the sudden sinking of her spirits.

Merrie wasn't quite sure what she felt for Dave Anders. She knew he was entirely the wrong sort of man for her, but she couldn't deny the attraction. And didn't chemistry like that at least deserve some experimentation?

As Merrie pulled into her driveway, Grandma Netta came over to the car. "This must be my new great-granddaughter! Do you like the snow I ordered for you?"

"You did?" Steffie looked as if she weren't quite sure just how far a great-grandmother's powers extended.

"Well, more or less." Netta gave the child a big hug. "I sure wish I could play with you this afternoon, but I'm on my way over to my friend's house. She's got a four-wheel-drive, so we can get out for our caroling tonight even if the snow's real bad."

"That's okay. Aunt Merrie's going to show me the cats." Unsmiling, Steffie waved good-bye to Netta and followed Merrie into the house.

Warmth rolled over them as they scurried inside and closed the door on the swirling flakes. Merrie wondered how the house looked to her niece. Steffie was too young to realize how much love had gone into furnishing and decorating it, of course, but could she sense how welcome she was, how Merrie had thought all the while that someday a child would live here?

Until this moment, Merrie herself hadn't realized how often she had fantasized about nursery rhymes and picture books and *Sesame Street*. With a pang, she realized that it was likely to be some time before she had a child of her own. How was she ever going to give up Steffie after the holidays?

Snoozer was in his usual place in front of the stove. Homebody crouched over the food dish, crunching idly on a treat. Wanderer was nowhere in sight, but a trail of melting snow leading in from the cat door provided ample evidence that even he had taken refuge from the storm.

Gravely, Merrie introduced Steffie to the cats. The girl stared at them, half-afraid. "Do they like me?"

As if by way of an answer, Homebody paced toward them curiously. The gray striped cat was the friendliest of Merrie's companions; unlike the others, which had both been strays, she'd been acquired as a kitten from a litter someone had dumped on the steps of the animal clinic.

"Homebody likes being scratched behind the ears," Merrie prompted.

Steffie crouched down and reached one hand forward tentatively. The cat meowed and lowered her head. Stubby fingers found the base of the ears and poked around. A rumble of satisfaction rose from the cat.

Startled, Steffie jumped back. "What's the matter?"

"She's purring. That means she's happy."

"Oh." With growing confidence, Steffie scratched Homebody again and smiled timidly as the rumbling intensified.

Merrie let them get acquainted for a while, then showed Steffie up to the guest bedroom. Although it had been decorated in discreet earth tones, Merrie had added a ruffled pillow and a pot of African violets for the occasion.

The girl showed no reaction, which wasn't surprising. In Lizabeth's apartment, the child's room had been gussied up by a professional, with pink-checked bedspread and curtains, rainbows on the wall, a hanging soft-sculpture mobile and lots of other expensive touches that no doubt Steffie was forbidden to play with.

"Let's go eat," Merrie suggested after finding that the guinea pigs were asleep, and deciding not to make them cranky by waking them up to amuse the little girl. "It's after five o'clock."

Steffie shrugged. "I suppose."

Dinner was simple—a chicken casserole that Merrie reheated in the microwave, along with glazed carrots and glasses of milk for them both. Steffie picked at her food.

"Don't you like it? You can have a hamburger or peanut butter and jelly, if you'd rather."

"No. It's okay." Steffie made a show of sticking some food in her mouth. She was much too thin. Perhaps Lizabeth, who was always on a diet herself, didn't realize that children needed good nourishment.

Merrie produced yogurt bars for dessert, and Steffie ate hers with a bit more interest. It was after six o'clock. Two more hours until Dave would come—if he came at all.

Outside, the snow was really piling up. Nashville didn't usually have more than a couple of heavy snowstorms during a winter. Merrie supposed it could be considered fortunate that this one had arrived in time for Christmas, but she wished it had held off for a few hours.

Steffie lay down for a nap without protest, which

gave Merrie a chance to mix up the batter for cookies. She kept the radio on, listening to reports of the accumulation.

The snow was stopping, the announcer said, although by now it was too dark out for Merrie to see much. But there was at least six inches of the stuff on the ground—more in some areas—and Nashville was pretty well shut down for Christmas Eve.

Dropping into a chair, Merrie bit the inside of her cheeks to stop the unexpected tears. It was ridiculous to feel so disappointed, whether for Steffie's sake or her own.

From here, she could see the lights of the Christmas tree twinkling against their reflection in the front window. Piled beneath were the gifts she'd bought for Steffie and the one for Dave.

For the first time since she'd moved in here, the house felt lonely. That was ironic, since, for a change, Merrie wasn't alone. But she'd been so busy with her work and volunteer activities and visits with Grandma Netta, that she hadn't really noticed the absence of a man.

Not just any man: one with a lively temperament who could veer from arrogance to amusement in the blink of a gray eye; one who talked to his collie; and dressed up as Santa Claus; and didn't hesitate to come to the rescue of a small boy on the street.

Merrie started from her reverie at a creak from the stairs. Steffie was staring around in confusion, as if she'd forgotten where she was.

"Good. You're up." Merrie quashed her own sadness, putting on a bright face for the child. "Let's make cookies."

"How do you make cookies?"

No doubt Steffie believed the things grew in bags in the grocery store. "I'll show you."

Getting the dough ready first might have been cheating, Merrie reflected as she helped Steffie shape cookies on wax paper, but she wasn't sure how much of an attention span a five-year-old had.

"Now here's the special part." Merrie extracted from a drawer the metal cookie cutters that Grandma Netta had given her years ago. There were a star and a bell and a cone-shaped tree. "See, you press them into the dough like this."

Soon Steffie was absorbed in the process of cutting out cookies and sprinkling them with tiny colored candies. Just as they tucked two trays into the oven, Merrie heard something very odd indeed.

Sleigh bells.

"That must be Santa Claus," Steffie advised her solemnly.

"Well . . . maybe." She hoped the child wouldn't be too let down. It was probably just some of the neighbors celebrating the holiday.

And then they both heard it: a loud "ho ho ho" from the street.

"It *is* Santa!" For the first time since she'd arrived, Steffie's face lit up.

Together, they ran to the front window. Sure enough, there, outside in the snow was a sleigh pulled by two hard-breathing horses, driven by Santa and a full-size elf.

"I don't believe it," Merrie muttered to herself. "Where did he get that thing?" She roused in time to stop Steffie from racing out into the snow without a coat. "Wait till he comes inside, sweetheart."

"But he might not know I'm here!" Steffie hopped up

and down and hollered out the door with uncharacteristic boldness: "Santa! Here I am!"

"Ho ho ho!" Santa climbed down from the sleigh, carrying his bag of gifts. Faces appeared in windows along the block. Chortling cheerily, Santa and his elf distributed gifts to the neighbors' children before the big red fellow turned toward Merrie's house. Silently, she thanked him for thinking of the other children who might be watching and who would have been hurt if they'd been overlooked.

"He's coming!" Steffie let out a squeal. "I've been good, Aunt Merrie! I've been good!"

"I'm sure you have." Opening the door, Merrie smiled at the jolly figure ambling toward her, wondering if Dave could tell how glad she was to see him, in or out of his disguise.

"And is there a little girl in here?" Stamping the snow from his feet on the front mat, Santa came into the house. His elf friend had returned to the sleigh.

"Santa! Santa!" Steffie ran up to him, fearlessly grabbing at a red-covered leg. "How come you didn't come down the chimney?"

"What? And get soot all over my nice clean clothes?" Dave knelt on the carpet and rummaged through his bag. "Now let me see—what have I got here . . ."

"I think you left a few things earlier," Merrie prompted, fetching the packages from under the tree. "Remember, you asked me to keep them till Christmas Eve?"

"So I did, but there's something else—here it is!" A bright foil-wrapped package came out of the bag. "And the name on it is—Steffie!"

"He knows my name!" Steffie clutched the package. "Aunt Merrie, he knows who I am!"

Dave sniffed the air. "Smells like somebody's baking something nice for Santa."

"The cookies!" Merrie dashed into the kitchen and retrieved them, just in time. "Why don't you invite your elf friend to come in, too?"

Santa and Steffie followed her into the kitchen. "He's got some errands to run. Got to keep the horses moving, as you ought to know, Doc. He'll be back. After all, this little girl flew all the way from New York. I can't just gobble down a few cookies and run, now can I?"

"But, Santa." The little girl's face grew solemn again. "What about all the other children in the world? If you stay here, how will they get their toys?"

"Oh, I have lots of helpers." Dave waved his hand airily. "All over the world, delivering toys in Hong Kong and Bermuda, Paris and Tokyo, wherever little children live."

"Are there any places where they don't have little children?" Steffie accepted a bell-shaped cookie and bit into it without even seeming to see it.

"Antarctica." From under his bushy white eyebrows, Dave shot Merrie a look of mock despair, as if he doubted he could dream up answers as fast as Steffie could think up questions.

"Aren't you going to open your presents?" Merrie asked her.

"Oh!" Tearing at the bright wrapper, Steffie produced a wrinkly-faced stuffed puppy, with a tiny matching companion. "Oh, look, it's got a baby! And it's going to take good care of its baby, too. It won't ever leave it or give it away, will it, Aunt Merrie?"

"Not ever." She knelt beside the child, tears in her eyes, and gave Steffie a big hug.

Dave's frown told her he didn't understand exactly what was going on. She'd only told him that Steffie was her niece. Well, explanations would have to wait.

With a little encouragement, Steffie opened her other gifts. She beamed at Big Bird, the crayons, and the books. But Dave's present was obviously her favorite. She played with the pups and sipped at hot chocolate as the grown-ups shared coffee and cookies, and the cats dozed around them.

Finally, Merrie remembered something. "And I've got a present for Santa, too." She retrieved his package from under the tree.

"Well, well." Dave quirked an eyebrow, finished his fifth cookie—or was it his sixth?—and examined the wrapping paper. "Now what can this be? Magic dust to make my elves work harder? Or maybe it's beard cleaner. I could really use some beard cleaner."

Steffie giggled. "Maybe it's something to feed your reindeer. I mean, horses. How come—"

Quickly, Dave tore upon the package to forestall the question. "Well, look here! A pooch!"

"That's cute!" Steffie looked down at her own wrinkled puppies. "Maybe he's the daddy. Do you think he's the daddy?"

Dave pretended to study the dogs carefully, even though the collie didn't look anything like the pups. "Could be. There's a lot science doesn't know. Eh, Doc?"

"I think he very well could be the daddy." Merrie wondered if Steffie would insist that Dave bring his stuffed collie back to visit, and realized she was hoping he would. Reluctantly, she noted that he'd been here over an hour, and wondered whether his friend would return soon.

Dave must have noticed her glancing at her watch; he got up and went to the door, peering out into the blackness. "Looks like it's started snowing again."

Joining him in the doorway, Merrie saw that the night had turned almost white. "Snowing isn't the word for it. This is a blizzard."

She flipped on the radio. After a few minutes, the Christmas music stopped and the announcer informed them that several more inches of snow had fallen in the last half hour. "This is the biggest storm Nashville's had in recent memory. I hope you're all snuggled under your comforters with a cup of hot cocoa and visions of sugar plums dancing through your heads." With that, he began to play Tchaikovsky's *Nutcracker Suite*.

"Maybe Santa had better telephone his elf," Dave murmured. He jerked his head meaningfully toward Steffie, who was yawning. "Looks like somebody might need to hit the hay."

It certainly wouldn't do for Steffie to overhear Santa discussing such practicalities as how to get rescued in a snowstorm. Merrie ushered her young charge up to bed. Steffie protested weakly, but the long day had exhausted her, and she fell asleep as soon as Merrie tucked her in, the wrinkled pups nestled in her arms and Homebody draped across her feet.

Dave hung up the telephone as Merrie came downstairs. "I had to call a few places to locate Kip—my elfin friend. He's at his sister's house, thrilling her kids. And it looks like he's going to be stuck there for the night."

"What about the horses?"

"Spoken like a veterinarian." He grinned under his white beard. "They'll have to make do with a garage and some carrots and apples."

"As long as everybody's safe. More coffee?" Merrie felt light-headed, as though someone had spiked the cookies. Usually her days were firmly anchored in schedules and responsibilities. Tonight she felt transported to a freer, younger, timeless world.

"Sure." Dave pulled off his cap and beard, and scratched his head with an expression of pure bliss. "That stuff doesn't feel bad when you're outside in the cold, but inside it's like wearing a horse blanket over your head."

"Speaking of horses, where did you get the sleigh?" Merrie fixed the coffee and set out the last of the cookies.

"Kip's a set designer." Dave helped her carry the mugs to the table, stepping carefully over Snoozer. "Works for Opryland and a lot of country singers when they're going on tour. He collects props. He's used the sleigh a couple of times—it's an old one, from Germany."

"It's beautiful . . ." Merrie's voice trailed away as she found herself trapped between Dave and the table. Gazing directly into her eyes, he began humming an unfamiliar tune. "What's that? The song, I mean." Her mind felt fogged in.

"It's an old classic. 'I Saw Mommy Kissing Santa.'" His lips descended on hers.

The kiss was so unexpected that for a moment she couldn't move. Then she didn't want to move.

Even through the pillow strapped around his waist, she could feel the hardness of Dave's body and the strength of his arms. His mouth was firm and questing, probing hers with a gentle playfulness that inspired her to respond in kind. Merrie tasted the minty sweetness of his mouth and brushed her nose against his warm cheek.

"You feel like a big teddy bear in that costume," she murmured.

"That wasn't exactly the response I was hoping for." He heaved an exaggerated sigh and stepped back to look at her. "You, on the other hand, look and smell absolutely delicious."

"It was really kind of you to come tonight." Sleepily, she leaned against him. "And you went to a lot of trouble to get that sleigh. I would have been so disappointed . . ." She hadn't meant to say that. "For Steffie's sake, I mean."

"Oh, I don't mind. As long as I'm fed well." Dave traced a finger along Merrie's cheekbone. "What do you usually eat for breakfast?"

"Breakfast?" She blinked. He was making one heck of an assumption! "Wait a minute. Just because I kissed you—"

"Merrie, my pet—you don't mind my reference to your profession, do you?—well, my pet, it doesn't seem to have occurred to your slightly addled brain that Santa is sleeping over tonight because Santa can't get home."

Merrie could feel the blush creeping along her cheekbones. She was the one who'd made the outrageous assumption. And it was true, she hadn't been thinking straight or she would have realized . . .

"You can't wear that tomorrow!" She poked at Dave's pillow-swelled belly. "You'll destroy Steffie's illusions." Then something else struck her. "Sleep over? But Steffie's in the guest room. I guess the couch—but Grandma Netta will probably be over first thing and—no, she must be stuck, too—" She stared at him helplessly, her thoughts too tangled to unsort.

"Are you always this confused, Doc?" Dave was watching her with amused disbelief.

"Only off duty," she admitted.

Finally, it dawned on her that he could sleep downstairs on the couch. The Santa costume could be safely stowed in a plastic trash bag, and Dave would borrow an oversize man's bathrobe that Merrie sometimes wore around the house. They would explain to Steffie that he was a friend who'd been stranded by the snow and had taken refuge here after she went to bed. Fortunately, on Christmas morning it might not look odd for him to lounge around in his robe until his friend arrived with some clothes.

Merrie sighed as she made up the couch. "I hate fibbing, but you have to protect a child's illusions, don't you?"

Carrying a blanket from the linen closet, Dave said, "You never explained why your niece is spending Christmas with you. Where are her parents?"

"Her mother died soon after she was born. She wasn't married, and I guess the father skedaddled." Merrie poked through the linen closet. "I could have sworn there was a pillow."

"This one's fine." Dave reached into his costume and pulled out the one strapped to his waist. "So Steffie's an orphan, so to speak?"

"So to speak, yes." Merrie plumped up the pillow and slipped it into a case. "She lived with an aunt until the woman died a few months ago. The only other relative was a cousin, a bachelor who didn't want her. So he arranged for her to be adopted, and that's where my sister Lizabeth comes in."

Dave picked up the bathrobe Merrie had brought downstairs for him and stepped into the guest bathroom. "And where is Loving Mom Lizabeth on Christmas Eve?" he asked through the door.

"In Switzerland. Skiing."

"With her husband?"

"No husband."

"I don't mean to insult your sister—" From inside,

Merrie could hear the tantalizing sound of cloth slipping over skin. Dave Anders was undressing right there on the other side of a door, in her own house. She tried not to, but she couldn't help imagining what he must look like with those firm muscles and wide shoulders. "But didn't she think Steffie might need her?"

"Lizabeth doesn't think about what other people need."

The door swung open. The maroon velour bathrobe that hung so loose on Merrie's slender figure stretched snugly across Dave's broad frame, falling open at the chest to reveal softly curling brown hair. Merrie forced herself to look away, going over to smooth down the covers on the couch and then realizing that her action was more suggestive than she'd intended.

Dave leaned in the bathroom doorway, studying her. "You know, a person might think you'd never had a man stay over before."

"I haven't." At his raised eyebrow, Merrie added, "Not in this house. I was nearly engaged once, a long time ago, but he turned out to be the wrong man for me."

"Good thing you found out in time."

"Yes, it was." She would have liked to ask about his past, but it wasn't as if they were on such intimate terms. A few stolen kisses didn't exactly give her the right to poke into his romantic history.

Dave strolled across the room to the couch. He obviously felt quite at home as he sat down and patted the cushion beside him.

"No, thanks." Merrie hung back, wishing she didn't feel so awkward. "I'd better be getting to bed myself. If I know children, Steffie will be up early in the morning. Oh! I nearly forgot!" She scurried over to the sideboard and pulled out the stocking she'd hidden there, full of small gifts and candies.

Carrying it to the fireplace, Merrie looked around for some way to attach it. "I guess I need some tape."

"Here." Dave brought a roll from the kitchen, where he must have spotted it on the counter. "Allow me." Before she could object, he reached around Merrie and fastened the stocking to the mantle, keeping her trapped between his arms.

"Great." She ducked her head to avoid his eyes. "Now I'd better—"

"Mmm." His cheek rubbed across her hair. "You smell like Christmas."

"It's the tree."

"Merrie?"

"What?"

"You're the most unromantic woman I ever met." Chuckling, he brushed a kiss across the tip of her nose.

"I am?" She sighed: "Do I need lessons?"

"I know an excellent teacher." Dave nibbled at the sensitive lobe of her ear. "Lesson number one: Relax. Smell the smells. Taste the flavors. Stop fighting the messages your body is sending you. Ah. That's better."

Merrie swayed against him, her eyes half-closed. He felt so good, so sure and right . . .

Upstairs, Steffie groaned in her sleep.

Merrie jumped back. "I'd better go up and check on her."

Reluctantly, Dave released her. "That wasn't bad for your first lesson. But I can see your education has a long way to go."

"Good night." Suddenly self-conscious, Merrie hurried toward the steps, then paused. "Merry Christmas, Dave."

"Merry Christmas."

As she went up the stairs, she thought she heard him say, "Lesson number two. Never let a dangerous man into your house unless you plan to let him stay."

But she knew she couldn't have heard him correctly.

CHAPTER
Four

MERRIE AWOKE TO the tantalizing aroma of fresh-brewed coffee and maple syrup. Pancakes, she thought dazedly, with lots of fresh butter. Grandma Netta must be downstairs, bustling happily about on Christmas morning . . .

And then she remembered. Grandma Netta was undoubtedly snowed in at her friend's house. And everyone else was snowed out.

Except, of course, for Steffie. And Dave Anders, who right now must be making himself at home in Merrie's kitchen.

No. Impossible. Not the social lion of Nashville, head of a major corporation, the arrogant owner of Champion something-or-other. The man who, she could have sworn, thought pancakes were something you ordered in a restaurant if you couldn't get crepes.

She swung out of bed, sleepily pulling on her slippers and reaching for a dark blue robe, until it occurred to her foggy brain that she didn't want to go downstairs looking like this. Still not quite able to focus, she pulled a pair of jeans out of her closet, along with a fuzzy pink sweater.

There was no point in going overboard, but at least she could brush her hair and apply a touch of makeup, which was as much as she ever wore. Regarding herself in the mirror, Merrie noticed an unaccustomed sparkle to her eyes and a flush of pink on her cheeks. It must be that Christmas was inspiring her.

She paused in front of the closed door to her bedroom, her hand on the knob, as memories of last night flooded in. Dave touching her cheek; Dave kissing her lightly; Dave making some remark about being dangerous.

What on earth had she been thinking of, to melt into his embrace? They were wrong for each other, she'd sensed that the first time she saw him. And yet his appeal was undeniable.

It wasn't quite Franco all over again. Dave was infinitely warmer and more sympathetic, obviously a fan of children and animals. But he lived in a world that Merrie had no desire to inhabit, where who you were and what you wore mattered more than what was in your heart.

On the other hand, the aroma of sizzling bacon was wafting up the stairs, overcoming her resistance. And if she could be tempted so easily by a little food, how much less would she be able to stand against Dave's alluring presence?

Well, for today they were on her turf, and she could allow herself to enjoy Christmas. For Steffie's sake and her own. But that would be the end of it.

Trying to ignore the shadow that darkened her mood at the prospect of not seeing Dave again, Merrie pulled the door open and tiptoed down the hall to Steffie's room.

It was empty.

Merrie checked the bathroom, but it was vacant. Steffie must be downstairs. How were she and Dave getting on, left to their own devices?

As quietly as she could, Merrie padded down the

stairs, avoiding the fourth step from the bottom, which always squeaked.

A radio was playing Christmas carols softly in the background. From the kitchen came the murmur of voices.

Merrie crept closer. Why couldn't she make out any words? All she could hear were some growls, and then a sharp yipping noise. She moved forward until she could peer through the doorway.

Steffie and Dave were crouching on the floor, each manipulating a little stuffed dog. The collie—handled by Dave—was licking the wrinkled puppy, making soothing noises, while Steffie's pup barked happily. The little girl's unbrushed hair fell around her face, and her bathrobe had been buttoned incorrectly so that it gapped out, but there was no mistaking the radiance of her expression.

Merrie would have liked to stand there for hours, watching the child and the man communicate affection through the toys, but a timer buzzed on the stove and Dave sat back on his heels.

"Want to help me flip the pancakes?" he asked.

"Sure!" Hopping up, Steffie caught sight of her aunt in the doorway. "Good morning, Aunt Merrie! Look who came in to cook our breakfast!"

Wondering exactly how Dave had explained his presence, and particularly the bathrobe, Merrie gave the girl a hug. "Aren't we lucky?"

"He's got a dog just like Santa's!" Steffie continued. "Oh, let me!" She dashed to the stove, and Dave solemnly helped her slide a spatula under a pancake and turn it. The half-cooked batter landed in a jagged heap, and Steffie bit her lip as if expecting a scolding.

Instead, Dave said, "Oh, good. They hold the syrup better that way, don't you think?"

"Yeah. I can do them all that way. Look!" said Steffie, and proceeded to do just that.

Within a few minutes, they were digging into the bacon, coffee and pancakes—or rather, panheaps, as Dave dubbed them.

Steffie talked more between mouthfuls than she had in the entire time Merrie had known her. She rattled on about Dave—apparently he'd explained that he always came over to cook Merrie's breakfast on Christmas Day, and that he didn't like to put his clothes on until he'd eaten, so he simply came over in his bathrobe. To Steffie that seemed perfectly logical.

"Maybe we could borrow some clothes from one of the neighbors." Through the café curtains, Merrie could see the sun glistening on an unbroken expanse of snow. Obviously, Dave was going to be with them for at least the next few hours, and she doubted he would relish staying in her robe that long.

"I want to play in the park." Steffie took a drink of milk.

"The park?" Then Merrie understood. "We don't have to go to a park to play, sweetie. We can just go out in the yard."

"Okay." Steffie set the glass down and tackled another slice of bacon, holding it over her mouth and lowering it bite by bite. Not the best of table manners, Merrie reflected, but she didn't see any point in correcting the girl. After all, it was Christmas. Besides, if there was one thing Lizabeth was sure to teach, it was how to behave in society.

As soon as the last crisp bit had disappeared, Steffie bounded upstairs, assuring them both that she could dress herself right down to the snowsuit.

"If she dresses herself the way she buttoned her robe, we're in trouble," Merrie whispered.

"You could just wander up there in a bit to see if she needs help," Dave agreed. "But not yet."

"No, of course not. It's important for kids to try doing things themselves." Then Merrie realized that wasn't exactly what he'd meant.

She realized it from the intimate way he was regarding her over the rim of his mug, and at the same time she became aware of sensory details that she'd been trying to block out for the past half hour. Such as how her fingers could almost feel the silky chest hair revealed by the deep V of his bathrobe. Or how her nostrils twitched at the faint aroma of spicy after-shave lotion that clung to him from the previous day, enriched by his own lightly musky fragrance.

"Did you sleep well?" He asked the question innocently, but overtones clung to it nevertheless.

"Actually, yes." Merrie couldn't remember dreaming at all. "I thought I'd be up half the night checking on Steffie."

"Having a man downstairs ought to make you feel safe," Dave corrected. "On the other hand, that could be an illusion."

"Are you saying you could be hazardous to my health?"

"In some ways." He grinned, setting aside the mug. "None that you need to worry about."

Merrie decided not to pursue the subject, so she changed to a topic that was less emotionally charged. "You're terrific with Steffie. Most men wouldn't even think of getting down on the floor and playing with stuffed animals."

"It was her idea," Dave pretended to defend himself. "Honest."

"And she bought that explanation, about your coming over here every Christmas in your robe? It's ridiculous."

"Children have a logic of their own." Dave began stacking the dishes from where he sat. "I decided there was no point in trying to invent a story that would convince a grown-up."

"You wouldn't have to. Grown-ups don't believe in Santa Claus," Merrie pointed out.

"Most grown-ups also wouldn't believe that a man would be wandering around a woman's house in the morning wearing a bathrobe if nothing happened the night before."

It occurred to Merrie that things *were* going to look awfully strange to Grandma Netta. "Oh, no." She stood up. "My neighbor two houses over is about your size. He might have some old clothes he wouldn't mind lending."

"What's your hurry?" Dave lounged back in his chair, tilting it at a perilous angle. "Did I tell you how terrific you look in pink? I'd never have expected it, with all the red you've got in your hair."

"Lizabeth's a model and, well, I don't often take her advice, but she is perceptive about colors." Merrie hesitated, one hand resting on the back of her chair, then realized she'd been avoiding acknowledging his praise. "I mean, thanks. I'm not very good at receiving compliments, am I?"

"You could have been a model." Dave ignored her apology as his gaze trailed slowly down her body, and Merrie was embarrassed to feel herself respond with an enhanced awareness of every soft curve. He might almost have been caressing her neck, her shoulders, her ... No, she wasn't going to think about that. "You're really quite striking, and yet completely natural. Almost coltish sometimes."

"Well, gee, no need to inundate me with flattery." Merrie tried to dispel the mood with some light irony, but her voice caught.

"So. You could have been a model, but you chose to become a veterinarian." Dave gathered the dishes and stood up, brushing against Merrie as if by accident on his way to the sink. The heat of his body was tantalizing and reassuring at the same time.

"It was that or a pediatrician, and I wasn't quite up to that long a grind," she admitted. "And what about you? Did you ever think of *not* going into the family business?"

"Actually, yes." To her amazement, he began loading the dishwasher as if it were something he did every day. Which, considering his bachelor status, it might be. "I had quite a few offers after I got my M.B.A."

"From Harvard?" It was intended as a joke, but he nodded agreement. "Hey, you don't do things halfway, do you?"

"Not if I can help it." There seemed to be some deeper meaning to his words, but his face was averted as he stuffed silverware into the wire holder. "Anyway, my dad wanted me to come in with him, and I'm glad I did. It gave us a chance to get to know each other better, and then he died suddenly of a heart attack. If I'd gone to work somewhere else, I think I'd always have regretted it."

Merrie was impressed that Dave's priority wasn't on his achievements in building up the business, but on the opportunity it had given him to get closer to his father. But, she warned herself, men as successful as Dave didn't get there without a lot of drive and single-mindedness, not to mention long hours. She was seeing Dave today at his best, relaxed and mellow, but, in her experience, anyone as high-powered as he was must have a flip side.

"A penny for your thoughts." Dave closed the dishwasher and leaned against it, regarding her. "What did I say to bring on so many emotions? By the way, did anyone ever tell you that your face is transparent? I can see everything you're feeling."

Merrie felt the heat rise to her cheeks. "Oh . . . it's a long story. I'd better go up and check on Steffie."

She left quickly, without giving Dave a chance to stop her. Darn it, he was too perceptive for her own good.

All thoughts of Dave vanished as soon as she stepped into Steffie's room and found the little girl sitting placidly on the bed, pulling a sweatshirt down over what looked like a tutu. The only thing on the child's legs was a pair of thin tights.

"Where do you think you're going, to a ballet recital?" Merrie was torn between amusement and exasperation.

"Don't you like it?" Steffie peered up at her. "My ballet teacher says I'm the best student in my class."

"Yes, but I thought you wanted to play in the snow."

"That's why I'm putting on the sweatshirt," the child replied impatiently, as if explaining the obvious. "I want Dave to see my tutu."

Children have a logic of their own. How right you are, Dave. "Well, why don't you run downstairs and show it to him, and then we'll dress you in something warmer, okay?"

"Okay." Cheerfully, the little girl bounded out of the room, not even bothering to take off the sweatshirt.

I guess I don't know as much about children as I thought, Merrie reflected as she flipped through Steffie's closet for the pair of jeans she'd unpacked the night before. The child's energy, the nooks and crannies of her mind, all presented a far greater challenge than dealing with even the wiliest of runaway monkeys.

In a minute, Steffie was back, but it took longer than Merrie would have expected to dress her. For one thing, the once-silent child now chattered a mile a minute, explaining every garment's history to Merrie and asking endless questions. For another, Steffie was in constant motion, twitching, scratching, turning to look at something, and forcing Merrie to chase each limb before stuffing it into the appropriate sleeve or pants leg.

By the time they descended the stairs, Merrie half expected to see that Dave had grown a long white beard of his own.

Instead, she was startled to find him seated in front of the fireplace, fully dressed, in a heavy tweed coat and deerstalker hat, leather gloves, old-fashioned trousers and leather slipper-shoes, with a pipe clamped between his teeth. He was the very image of Sherlock Holmes.

"You look nice," Steffie said solemnly.

"Thank you, madam," Dave replied in a British accent.

"Where—" Merrie broke off the question. "It was in the back of the hall closet, wasn't it?"

"Along with another costume, but it looked too small," Dave said in his normal accent. "I'm almost afraid to ask what they're for."

"Last Halloween, my partner Bill and I thought the clients would enjoy it if we dressed up." Merrie smiled at the memory. "He was Sherlock Holmes and I was Dr. Watson. Everybody thought it was great, so I saved the costumes to use again next year."

"A bit tight through the shoulders, but not a bad fit." Dave crossed to the closet and extracted her ski jacket, helping her into it. "Now let me see. I deduce that you and Bill get along very well, but that he's married to someone else."

"Very good, Sherlock." Merrie adjusted Steffie's hood, tucking a strand of dark hair out of sight. "How did you figure that out?"

"Elementary, my dear Watson." Dave extracted a crumpled piece of paper from one pocket. It was a note asking Bill to pick up some groceries, and was signed, Love, Sue.

"Merrie's name isn't Watson," Steffie pointed out.

"We're playing a game." Merrie steered the child toward the door. "We're pretending to be characters from a book. Now let's go enjoy the snow, shall we?"

She swung the door open and inhaled the crisp pine-tinged fragrance of the morning. From down the street came the shouts of children, and telltale sled tracks crisscrossed in the middle of the street. But for the most part the snow was still unmarred, transforming the landscape of brick houses, bare trees, and parked cars into a gleaming fantasyland.

"The buildings are so short." Steffie stared down the street.

Dave laughed and swung the child up, drawing a snort of laughter from her. "This is Nashville, not New York. We have some skyscrapers, too, but we prefer to live in houses."

"Me, too." Steffie let out a whoop as he twirled her around. "Do that again!"

Watching the two of them whirl through the snow, Merrie felt her heart squeeze with nostalgia. She rarely thought about her own childhood; it seemed so long ago, as if it belonged to someone else. Now she realized that living with a child meant reliving, to a certain extent, one's own childhood. There had been days like this for her, too, while her father was alive, when a pair of strong arms and the swooping sensation of being hoisted above the snow were the most exciting things in the world.

But what she felt went beyond that. Her vague wish for a husband and family had honed itself into a sharp edge. *This* was what she wanted, this moment, this fragile sense of belonging and happiness. She wanted it to last forever, even though she knew it couldn't.

"Can we build a snowman?" Steffie was demanding. "Aunt Merrie?"

"Of course." Merrie roused herself at once. "It's been years since I've done that."

"We'll need the proper accoutrements—that is, gear," Dave added for the child's benefit. "I don't suppose you've got lumps of coal for the eyes, but perhaps a carrot for the nose?"

"And a hat!" Steffie added.

"Why don't we make the snowman before we worry about decorating him?" Merrie wadded up some snow into a ball and began rolling it through the yard.

"Lumpy." Dave regarded her with a mock-critical eye. "You'll never be able to make it big enough for the base."

"Let me try!" Steffie snatched at some snow, which crumbled in her mittens.

"Like this." Dave showed the child how to make a perfect round ball. Even Merrie had to admit that he knew what he was doing, and she abandoned her own lopsided effort.

It was remarkable to see how meticulous he could be in getting the shape right, and yet completely patient with Steffie's awkwardness. If he showed the same traits with his employees, it was no wonder his business had done so well.

Their snowman turned out to be quite a character. In addition to the traditional two-tiered body, he had legs and feet folded in front of him, and arms draped over his hips. They settled on prunes for the eyes, a carrot nose, and cranberries for the mouth, which at least would give the birds a meal. Some old brown yarn, cut into strands, served as hair.

A group of neighborhood children, tired of sledding, gathered around to watch and comment. Steffie jumped up and down, delighted by all the attention.

"Well," Merrie said as the others finally began to wander off, "who feels like a cup of hot chocolate?"

"Twist my arm." Dave dusted snow off his gloves.

"Why?" Steffie demanded. "Wouldn't it hurt?"

"What I meant was, she doesn't need to twist my arm." Dave winked at Merrie. "I can see I have to watch what expressions I use."

As they crunched their way to the back porch and began stomping off the snow, Merrie heard the distant sound of machinery. Snowplows.

That meant Grandma Netta would be home soon. Merrie would be glad to see her grandmother, but she couldn't help regretting the loss of their isolation. This morning had been magical, suspended in time, and she was in no hurry for it to end.

"Real hot chocolate?" Dave asked as they deposited their wet shoes inside the kitchen door. "Or that instant stuff?"

"Real hot chocolate," Merrie assured him. "But I want to get Steffie changed first. Her pants are soaked."

The little girl was quieter now, tired by her exertions, and soon they were all settled in front of a fire—Dave's contribution—with their hot chocolate, and Steffie was digging through the gifts in her stocking.

"I like it here," the child announced at last into the

companionable silence. "Can I come back to visit, Aunt Merrie?"

"I certainly hope so." She exchanged glances with Dave, and then heard the sound she'd been anticipating, the chug-clunk of an aging auto.

"Is that Grandma Netta?" Steffie bounced over to the window.

"I think so, sweetie." Merrie set her cup down and added for Dave's benefit, "My grandmother lives next door."

Dave joined Steffie at the window. "She looks just like a grandmother ought to. And she's coming this way." He glanced down at his Sherlock Holmes costume. "I suppose she might wonder what I'm doing in this."

Fortunately, Steffie was absorbed in her great-grandmother's approach and didn't bombard him with questions. Merrie shrugged. She'd told Netta that Dave would be here to play Santa Claus, and she suspected her grandmother could figure out the rest.

Netta must have stowed Steffie's gift in her car, because she didn't even bother to stop by her own house. Standing in the doorway, her cheeks bright red and her arms encircling a gaily wrapped package, she did indeed look the very picture of an old-fashioned grandmother.

"Merry Christmas!" Merrie gave her a hug. "We have a—uh—guest this morning." She shot Netta a look that, Merrie hoped, conveyed they weren't to discuss the matter in front of Steffie.

"Sherlock Holmes, I presume," Netta greeted Dave without batting an eye.

"He comes here every Christmas," Steffie volunteered. "In his bathrobe."

"Does he?" Netta lifted an eyebrow. "Well, now. Do you have a kiss for me, child?"

Merrie was grateful that, during the next few minutes, everyone's attention was taken up with hugs and opening the gift—a set of Peter Rabbit books, which Steffie crowed over joyfully. Then they had to hurry to catch the late service at the church down one block, and when they came home Netta bustled about helping Merrie prepare a light lunch of soup and French bread. But Merrie didn't suppose for one moment that her grandmother had missed anything of what was going on, or that there wouldn't be plenty of questions later.

"I heard Santa Claus paid you a visit last night," Netta remarked over her second cup of hot chocolate.

"He knew my name!" Steffie paused in slurping her soup. "And he brought me the cutest little puppies!" Sliding down from her chair, she dashed into the living room and returned with one. "See? And Dave has a collie just like Santa's. Isn't that funny?"

"I suspect Dave has a lot of things like Santa's," murmured Netta.

Feeling herself start to blush again, Merrie wondered if Netta had intended her remark to be as risqué as it sounded. She didn't dare look at Dave, who had accepted the entire scene with a façade of bland good nature that she suspected masked a great deal of amusement.

After a round of cookies, Netta excused herself. "I haven't been home since yesterday and frankly, I'm bushed. I'm getting too old for such shenanigans."

"You wouldn't give up your caroling?" Merrie was distressed at the idea. "You've always enjoyed it so much."

"Well, we'll see. I have a whole year to think it over." Netta buttoned up her coat and wrapped a knitted scarf around her head and neck. "Fortunately, it doesn't usually snow this hard on Christmas Eve."

After she left, Merrie surveyed the living room with its crumpled wrapping paper, empty hot chocolate mugs, and damp coats scattered about. "I think I'll set fire to the place." Then, remembering that Steffie tended to take things literally, she added, "Just joking."

The little girl yawned. "Can I have another cookie?"

"Yes, and then you can have a nap." Merrie escorted her upstairs, the cookie gripped tightly in the little fist. Despite her protests that she wasn't tired, Steffie's eyes closed as soon as her head touched the pillow, and within a minute her breathing was smooth and regular.

Downstairs, Dave had collected the mugs and was straightening up the kitchen.

"You're every woman's dream," Merrie told him as she began putting away the food.

"So I've been told," he replied promptly. "But not for my housekeeping talents."

Merrie refused to touch that one. "What are the transportation arrangements?"

"Are you trying to get rid of me?" He didn't wait for an answer. "Actually, I just called Kip and he'd left to take the horses home. I suspect I may have to call a cab."

"I can give you a ride as soon as Steffie wakes up." Merrie tucked the plastic-wrapped French bread into the refrigerator. "Where do you live?"

"Actually, I left my car at Kip's, but we both live in Belle Meade," he said. "And as long as we're out, why don't we take a tour of Nashville in the snow? I'll bet it's dazzling, and Steffie would enjoy it."

"Sure." Merrie couldn't find anything else that needed picking up or putting away. She felt awkward, facing Dave without the child here to keep them occupied. "Want another cup of something hot?"

"I'd rather take up where we left off last night." He leaned on the counter. "What is it about me that makes you uncomfortable?"

"The fact that you ask questions like that," she said.

"You'd rather talk about animals?" He gestured toward Snoozer, lying in a fluffy lump by the stove. "Or food, or just about anything else except what goes on between a man and a woman?"

"Now, look." Merrie injected as much firmness as she could into her voice. "We've had a good time, and you're a good sport, but—" She stopped, realizing she didn't know what came next. But what? How could she tell Dave that he was wrong for her, when she wasn't sure of that herself?

Why *did* he make her so uncomfortable? Maybe, she reflected ruefully, it was because, after Franco, she'd avoided men that weren't easily handled. Which Dave certainly wasn't.

"But you don't know me very well yet," he finished for her. "And I know the remedy for that. We'll just have to spend a lot of time together."

"Not right now," Merrie stalled. "Not over the holidays."

"We'll see about that." She hoped Dave couldn't perceive the surge of anticipation that his words evoked. "However, I'll be tied up for a few days—my mother's been in Florida for a week, so we're having a late Christmas celebration this weekend."

"Aunt Merrie?" The small voice came from the top of the stairs. "I woke up, and I can't get back to sleep. Can I come down?"

"Do you have your shoes on?" Relieved at the interruption, Merrie went to tend to Steffie. She supposed an abbreviated nap wouldn't do any harm. "Okay. We're going out to look at Nashville in the snow."

Dave was still stuck with his Sherlock Holmes jacket, but he didn't seem to mind. "I'll have this cleaned," was all he said, and gathered up the garbage bag in which they'd stowed the Santa Claus costume.

For a moment, as they settled into her car, Merrie was afraid it wouldn't start in the cold, but the engine caught after a moment and clouds of white steam billowed out behind them.

Steffie, seat-belted between them, noticed details of the city that Merrie rarely paid attention to: a brightly painted mailbox, an unusual storefront, a row of blackbirds on a telephone wire.

Nashville looked pristine and unfamiliar beneath its blanket of white, like a city one was revisiting after being away for years. It reminded Merrie of her homecoming from New York, of seeing Grandma Netta's house again and wondering if it had always looked so solid and timeless.

They drove past the large-scale replica of the Greek Parthenon in Centennial Park, but Steffie scarcely glanced at it. She was too busy watching a group of children sledding on the slopes nearby.

"I guess I don't really know what a child would like to see," Merrie admitted to Dave over the little girl's head. "I keep thinking about museums and stuff like that. Too bad Opryland's closed this time of year; she'd probably enjoy the music and the rides."

"Who needs them?" Dave gestured at the snow-blanketed Vanderbilt University campus as they cruised by. "The whole world's a wonderland."

After about an hour of touring the city, they were all feeling cramped and a bit steamed out from the car heater. "I know what I want to see!" Steffie cried.

"What?" Merrie blew on her fingers, which the heater hadn't quite reached.

"McDonald's!"

"I'm sure Steffie's interest is purely cultural," Dave added. "It's those artistic golden arches."

"Right." Merrie kept a tight grip on the wheel as the little girl squirmed delightedly beside her.

They trooped into the McDonald's near Merrie's house and settled down with hot drinks and French fries. Despite her obvious weariness, Steffie beamed. "I like Nashville."

"I guess so." Merrie squeezed her arm around the child's shoulders. "And I think it likes you."

"Maybe I'll come back a lot." Steffie frowned. "Next week."

"You'll still be here next week."

"Okay, the week after that."

There was no point correcting the little girl. Besides, Merrie realized, she would like it very much if Steffie came back often. And the week after next wouldn't be too soon.

They dropped Dave off at Kip's house, an unusual home set into the side of a hill. Under other circumstances Merrie would have coveted a look inside, but Steffie was yawning and, besides, Kip wasn't expecting visitors.

"I'd invite you over to my place, but I think Sleeping Beauty needs the rest of her nap." Dave kissed the top of Steffie's head. "Sweetie, I may not see you again before you leave, but I'll make sure to be around next time you're in Nashville."

"Okay," the child murmured, half-asleep.

Dave caught Merrie's gaze and held it briefly. "I'll be seeing you," he said quietly.

Watching him stride away with the garbage bag slung

over one shoulder, Merrie realized that she was glad. Glad he'd come to her house, glad he'd stayed overnight, and glad she'd be spending more time in his company. Even if she must be crazy to allow it.

"Let's go home," she said to the dozing child, and backed out of the driveway.

CHAPTER
Five

THE ORIGINAL PLAN had been for Steffie to stay through New Year's Day, so Merrie had mixed feelings when a telegram arrived telling her that Lizabeth would arrive on Tuesday, only four days after Christmas.

"What do you suppose it means?" She picked at her second slice of Netta's fabulous fruitcake. In her grandmother's living room, Steffie was chortling at the Monday morning antics of Oscar the Grouch on *Sesame Street*.

"Well . . ." Netta stared down at her square-tipped fingers as if to find some inspiration there. "It *might* mean she misses the child terribly and is stricken by pangs of guilt."

"It also might mean the Swiss chalet burned down and the hotels were all booked up." Merrie swallowed a candied cherry. "Sorry. That was cruel, wasn't it?"

"Just realistic." Netta shook her head. "I never understood your mother, and I'll never understand your sister, either. If I had a daughter like Steffie . . . but that's neither here nor there. By the way, have you seen any more of that Anders fellow?"

"You know I'd have told you." Merrie refrained from adding that she was grateful her grandmother hadn't presumed the worst about what had happened Christmas Eve. Merrie had always told Netta the truth, and obviously her grandmother knew it. "Well, I have to get to the clinic. I really appreciate your looking after Steffie while I'm at work."

"Believe me, I'd be offended if you hadn't asked." Netta tossed down her napkin. "Have a good day. Help lots of animals."

But throughout that day, and the next, Merrie had a hard time concentrating on her work.

Dave was a major part of the problem. Not that he called her or showed up; he apparently was devoting himself to his mother. But a part of him remained with her, like a tantalizing scent that haunted every room she entered.

When Merrie checked the animal cages, she saw his lean body bending to greet his collie, or dashing across to help capture an errant monkey.

At home, his smile hung in the air like the Cheshire cat's. How had he come to be so much a part of her world in so short a time?

Then, when she did manage to push Dave from her thoughts for a brief span, Lizabeth intruded. Stunning ash-blond Lizabeth, always the focus of attention, her laugh a trifle premeditated, her head tossing so the light fell across her face at just the right angle. Even when she wasn't modeling, Lizabeth was always on camera.

Merrie didn't doubt that, in her own careless way, Lizabeth was fond of Steffie. The three of them had gone shopping together during Merrie's Thanksgiving visit to New York, and both the child and her newfound mom had gotten a kick out of trying on mother-and-daughter outfits, giggling together in a way Merrie couldn't help envying.

But Lizabeth hated to be inconvenienced, and for her, out of sight generally meant out of mind unless she needed a favor. What could have happened that was so important she was flying back early from Switzerland,

and why hadn't she mentioned it in her telegram?

It was hard not to communicate her anxiety to Steffie, but Merrie did her best. The little girl's face fell when she learned her visit apparently would be cut short, but she did seem eager to see Lizabeth again.

On Tuesday afternoon, Merrie took off an hour early from work to drive to the airport. She'd decided it might be a good idea to greet Lizabeth alone, so they could talk freely.

As always, Lizabeth was one of the first passengers to debark, since she traveled first class. Her hair falling freely about the shoulders of her ski sweater, she looked the very picture of youth as she strode through the welter of passengers, ignoring the heads that turned to watch.

"Merrie!" Lizabeth pressed a prefunctory kiss on her sister's cheek. "You look wonderful! But you smell like—"

"My last patient was an overly friendly cocker spaniel," Merrie admitted ruefully as she guided her sister toward the escalator. "I did my best to clean up, but I was afraid I'd be late."

"Well, there are worse smells than dog." Lizabeth glanced around. "Have they been adding on to this airport? It looks different."

"Yes, as a matter of fact." Mentally conceding the impossibility of conducting a serious discussion until they were settled, Merrie chatted on about inconsequentials as they found a skycap to collect her sister's designer luggage and made their way out to the car.

Four days of hard wear had reduced the snow to bits of slush and a few brownish drifts. "White Christmas?" Lizabeth scraped off her elegant leather half-boots before sliding into the car.

"Very." Merrie settled beside her. "What are you in

the mood to eat tonight? We could pick up something on the way home."

"Sushi?" Lizabeth finished buckling her seat belt. Her greatest fear was that something would damage her looks, so Lizabeth always took safety precautions. "No, not in Nashville, I don't suppose."

"Hamburgers?"

Lizabeth made a face. "You've been corrupting Steffie, haven't you? Or letting her corrupt you. Oh, well, how about pizza? I can indulge; I lost a couple of pounds on the slopes. Do you know, there's a place in Los Angeles that serves the most marvelous pizza, with duck, mussels, whatever you like. Simply *everyone* goes there."

"How about pepperoni?" Merrie said, and was relieved when her sister consented.

Lizabeth's high-spirited chatter filled the car as they drove. Her sister was in a fine mood and at her most charming, which was very charming indeed, Merrie had to admit. There was no one more entertaining than Lizabeth when she felt like it.

It wasn't until after they'd stowed the pizza safely in the back seat that Merrie finally brought up what was on her mind. "I take it you have some good news."

"Well, yes. Terrific news, actually." Lizabeth paused dramatically, no doubt to let the tension build, and it worked. Was it a movie contract? Had she started a clothing line? Finally, she broke the suspense by announcing, "I'm getting married!"

Fortunately, they were sitting at a red light, so Merrie didn't have to concentrate on traffic. This was the last thing she'd expected. "Anyone I know?" was all she could think to ask.

"No. We've been dating on the sly—he can't stand gossip. Then we went away to Switzerland as sort of a test, and pow! We realized we were made for each other." Lizabeth leaned toward Merrie. "You'll be so impressed. You can't imagine how rich he is! And from old money, even though he's made plenty of his own. He's fun to be with, too, in a low-key sort of way. But then, that's what I need. Stability. Come on, even you have to agree with that!"

"I hope he'll be a good father for Steffie." It was the first thing that popped into Merrie's mind, but then she realized how ungracious that might sound. "I mean, congratulations, Liz. You know I want you to be happy."

"I know." Her sister leaned back in her seat, wearing a positively euphoric grin. "And I will be. He really is the right man, Merrie. I've been invited to meet his family in Boston over New Year's. Oh, I'm so nervous! Imagine, me, marrying into an old family like that! I don't suppose they're thrilled about Drum marrying a model—that's his name, Drummond Haymes III—but then, his first wife was from Boston society, and it was a catastrophe! The only good thing was that they had two children, which means he doesn't want any more."

"Not even Steffie?" Merrie asked as she pulled into her driveway.

"Oh, well, he knows she's a fact. But we can discuss that later!" Lizabeth swung her door open. "I can't wait to see Grandma! Did I tell you I dropped by Mom's place on the Riviera, with Drum? She absolutely adored him, but then, she and I think alike. Our stepfather was off in Italy somewhere; he and Gigi seem to like taking time apart. *Chacun à son gout.*" Without waiting for a reply, she charged forward toward Netta's house, leaving Merrie to bring in the pizza.

It wasn't until late that evening, settled in Merrie's

living room with snifters of amaretto, that they had another chance to talk privately.

Steffie had greeted Lizabeth with a mixture of eagerness and uncertainty that tore at Merrie's heart. Instinctively, she felt that the child didn't know where she stood.

But they'd all enjoyed the pizza, and Lizabeth had regaled them with tales of the famous and infamous she'd seen on the Swiss slopes. It was after eleven now, and an exhausted Steffie had been tucked into bed an hour ago.

"I could see what Grandma was thinking." Lizabeth's slightly husky voice broke the silence. "She thinks I'm marrying Drum for his money."

"Of course you're not," Merrie said loyally. "For one thing, you earn plenty of your own."

"Let's be honest here." Lizabeth lounged along the couch Cleopatra-style, one arm draped over the back. "Would I marry him if he were poor? Don't be ridiculous. Pinching pennies has never been my style."

Knowing her sister needed no prompting, Merrie sipped wordlessly at the almond-flavored liqueur. It felt strange to see Lizabeth reclining on the same couch where Dave had sat only a few nights before. With a pang, she realized that she missed him, and ruthlessly pushed the thought from her mind.

"On the other hand, I've met a lot of wealthy men, and quite a few of them wouldn't mind having a beautiful wife to dangle in front of their friends." Lizabeth had no false modesty. "But I have no intention of being some old man's plaything. Drum's not like that."

"I can't wait to meet him," Merrie said. "Have you set a date?"

"Not until after I meet his family. But soon." Lizabeth tapped her fingers on the back of the sofa. "I'm not foolish enough to think they'll approve of me; I just hope they don't disapprove. Not that it would change Drum's mind, but it could make things unpleasant. Oh, Merrie, I'm so happy! You can't imagine how perfect he is. Well, almost."

The *almost* made Merrie's breath catch in her throat. Why did she think it had something to do with Steffie? But then, Lizabeth *had* mentioned that he didn't want children.

"You see, Drum is head of the Haymes Hotel chain, in case you hadn't recognized the name." Lizabeth dismissed that possibility with a wave of the hand. Clearly she thought Drummond Haymes was a household word. "He travels a lot, checking out the hotels, seeking new locations—I suppose you know their newest hotel is almost completed right here in Nashville. Well, not quite their newest; they're building one in Hong Kong, but it's still in the planning stages."

Merrie wasn't about to let her sister get sidetracked. "So he travels a lot."

"Well, yes, and naturally I'd want to go with him. Of course, that doesn't mean I'm abandoning my career." Lizabeth swung her long legs down and leaned across the coffee table to refill her glass. "As you know, I've had a couple of small roles in TV, and that's the direction I'm headed in. We're looking for the right property."

So Drum was going to stake his new wife to a Hollywood career. Well, who could blame him? Merrie had to admit that her sister was stunning, and plenty of models had made the transition successfully, from Cybill Shepherd to Jessica Lange. "So where does Steffie fit into the picture?"

"Now, Merrie, don't get all huffy." Lizabeth tucked an errant strand of blond hair behind her ear. "I know you didn't think I should have adopted her in the first place, but I have, and I'm not shirking my responsibility."

Steffie isn't just a responsibility! She's a child, and she deserves your love, not your duty! But Merrie bit her lip and waited.

"So anyway, about Steffie. I've talked it over with Drum, and we don't feel that's any life for a child, being shuffled from one hotel to another. Besides, she'll be six next fall, which means she needs to start school, and of course we can't be dragging her out of class all the time." Lizabeth hesitated, obviously nervous about her sister's reaction, then plunged ahead. "So we're looking for a good boarding school. The best. Of course, she'll spend summers and holidays with us, or occasionally with you, if you don't mind. I mean, only if I'm just absolutely tied up with shooting a picture or something."

Merrie took a deep breath to keep from exploding. Of all the insensitive, selfish things her sister had done, this was the worst. To stick a young child like Steffie in boarding school!—and with her background of painful separations, too. "Don't you think she's a little young for that? I had the impression even the British aristocracy didn't send their kids away until they were eight or so."

Lizabeth, who was usually refreshingly blunt, for once didn't answer directly. "Now, don't worry, I'm not going to snatch her away from you just yet. In fact, I hoped you wouldn't mind keeping her here for a few more weeks. I doubt if she'd enjoy the trip to Boston. Frankly, I'm not expecting to enjoy it myself."

"Of course she can stay here." And with those words, an idea popped into Merrie's head that seemed so perfectly logical, she couldn't imagine why she hadn't thought of it immediately. "Lizabeth, why don't you let Steffie stay with me? I mean, next year, while she's in school. We have some excellent schools—public or private, whatever you prefer—right here in Nashville, and I'd love to have her. And I'll bet Grandma Netta wouldn't mind baby-sitting after school, so she'd be well supervised." She paused to catch her breath, fighting the desire to press on and on until her sister gave in from sheer exhaustion.

"I was afraid you'd say something like that." Lizabeth's shapely mouth twisted in dismay. "Merrie, you're wonderful with children and animals, no question about it, but I want Steffie to grow up with a sense of discipline and ... values. No offense intended, but you and I have very different lifestyles." Her sister's gaze swept the living room—the stuffed animals and picturebook sprawled on the carpet, the Christmas tree listing slightly to one side with its ornaments disarranged by a child's hands, and Homebody curled on a chair, which was by now nearly as covered with gray cat fur as the cat herself. "I suppose it would be different if you were more settled—married, that sort of thing—but let's face it, you're just not the type."

"Not the type to get married?" Merrie repeated blankly. "What's that supposed to mean?"

"You're too—strong-willed. You don't know how to cater to a man." Lizabeth caught herself up short. "Honey, I didn't mean to turn this into a critique session. I like you just the way you are. But this environment isn't, well ... stable enough for Steffie."

Merrie knew her sister well enough to translate the message: *stable* meant not only settled, but also socially acceptable. On the other hand, the fact that Lizabeth didn't want to come right out and acknowledge her snobbery might make her own words an effective tool to use against her. "But if I *were* married, you'd feel differently?"

"Of course. Unless he was some hippie-type or something." Lizabeth relaxed, as if believing the conversation at an end. "But it's pointless to speculate, don't you think?"

The remark about her being too strong-willed to marry still rankled, and Merrie blundered on without giving herself time to reflect. "Actually, I hadn't meant to tell you because we haven't announced it yet, but I *am* thinking of getting married." A warning bell went off in her brain. Wait a minute—she hadn't really said that, had she? "I mean . . . well . . . it isn't official or anything . . ."

"Merrie! You sly fox!" Lizabeth clinked her glass down on the table. "Now, come on. Who is it? Does Grandma Netta know?"

Merrie shook her head and wondered how she was going to get herself out of this one. On the other hand, a make-believe engagement—with the man conveniently out of sight—might turn out to be useful, if she could pull it off. "Nobody does. But he loves Steffie. Of course, we probably won't actually get married right away, but you see, I am changing. Becoming more settled, you might say. So Steffie could—"

"What's his name?" Lizabeth wasn't about to be put off. "Not that veterinarian partner of yours?"

"Bill? He's quite happily married already." Now how was she going to put off Lizabeth's questions without losing all chance of winning permission to keep Steffie? "I don't think he'd like for me to tell you. I suppose you could say that, like Drum, he hates gossip."

"I know!" Lizabeth's eyes glowed a deep azure. "That man Grandma Netta mentioned, the one who was here on Christmas! Dave Anders. I think Gigi—she

doesn't like to be called Mom anymore, you know—
went to school with his mother. Oh, she'll be delighted!
I can't wait to tell her!"

"Lizabeth! I said it's a secret." Too late, Merrie remembered that one of her sister's greatest weaknesses
was her love of being first with a piece of gossip.

"I'm impressed," Lizabeth crowed. "He sounds like
a dream. Rich—from old Nashville society—perfect.
If Steffie's going to be moving in those circles, I certainly wouldn't object to her living here."

It was that last sentence that stifled the protests bub-
bling to Merrie's lips. "You mean you'd let her stay
with me? Even though we probably won't be getting
married for—for quite a while?"

"Well, I'm not promising anything yet, but I might."
Lizabeth regarded her with a smug look. "So you've
been keeping this under your hat, have you? It took Big
Sis to drag it out of you. Merrie, you're amazing. Anyone else would be shouting it from the rooftops."

"I told you, Dave doesn't want any gossip." Heaven
help me if he ever gets wind of this, Merrie thought
with a lurch of dismay. But how *was* she going to manage the logistics? Lizabeth would certainly expect to see
Dave from time to time, wouldn't she? Unless, of
course, she was too busy traveling with Drum.

Her sister's next words put an end to that hope. "I've
been thinking—maybe Drum and I should get married
here in Nashville. I don't particularly want to have a
wedding on his family's turf, and the new hotel has a
lovely ballroom. Maybe you and your fiancé could be in
the wedding party. What do you think?"

Oh, what a tangled web we weave . . . "It sounds . . .
wonderful." There was nothing further Merrie could do
tonight to extricate herself, she realized with a pang.
What she needed was to give the matter some hard

thought. "You must be exhausted after your flight."

"I slept on the plane." Lizabeth only needed about five hours of sleep a night; as a teenager, Merrie had sometimes suspected her sister came from another planet. "But I *am* getting sleepy. Well, okay. We'll talk some more in the morning. And congratulations."

Congratulations. The word rang in Merrie's ears as she checked on Steffie—something that Liz didn't think to do—and changed into her nightgown.

What on earth had she gotten herself into?

CHAPTER
Six

UNFORTUNATELY, A NIGHT of thinking things over failed to make a dent in Merrie's problem. She'd told a flat-out lie, and now she was going to have to own up to it.

She wouldn't have minded so much for herself. The problem was Steffie.

Watching the little girl tussle with the cats after breakfast, hearing her bright laughter as she went for a walk with Lizabeth the next morning, Merrie's heart twisted in pain at the thought of Steffie being consigned to a boarding school. Perhaps it wouldn't be so bad later on, when she could enjoy the special activities offered: horseback riding, elaborate art classes, that sort of thing. But not yet.

Besides, I'd miss her too much.

Lizabeth was set to leave for Boston that afternoon, and, fortunately, Bill had agreed to cover for Merrie at the clinic, since business was slow over the holidays. While mother and daughter were out on their walk, Merrie hurried next door to confer with Grandma Netta.

Over mugs of orange-spice tea, she confessed what she'd done. "And now I guess I've got to tell her the truth. But it's tearing me apart."

"I'm ashamed of my granddaughter." Netta bit down on the words with unaccustomed ferocity.

"Oh, Netta, I'm sorry..."

"I don't mean you. I mean that self-centered sister of

yours." The older woman glared at an inoffensive Smoky Mountains calendar on the wall. "Put the child in boarding school, indeed! Lizabeth *deserves* to be lied to."

This was a response Merrie hadn't expected. "But I couldn't keep it up. She'll want to meet Dave—"

"Then you'll have to let him in on it." Netta pushed forward a plate of bran muffins, and Merrie took one automatically.

"You've got to be kidding." She hardly tasted her mouthful of muffin, even though her grandmother was one of the world's best bakers. "That's outrageous."

"It might appeal to his sense of humor." Netta rested her chin on the palm of her hand. "Of course, there could be complications, but I don't suppose it's anything the two of you can't handle. He does seem fond of Steffie."

Merrie couldn't believe they were discussing this seriously, but since they were, they might as well look at all the angles. "Lizabeth's talking about getting married in Nashville. If she does, she'll be hanging around for quite a while, and I don't see how we could keep up the pretense."

Netta chuckled. "Lizabeth? Get married in Nashville? Nonsense. It's not—what's the word they love in the magazines—'tony' enough. Oh, no, if it isn't to be some big Episcopal church in Boston or New York, it'll be the Riviera or Malibu. Mark my words."

Merrie began to relax. "You really think so?"

"I'm sure of it."

Feeling better than she had in the last day and a half, Merrie slipped back into her house before her sister and Steffie returned. Maybe it really wouldn't be so complicated, after all. Dave might even regard it as kind of a joke. And it was true that Lizabeth hardly ever came to Nashville these days.

The hours until Lizabeth's flight passed quickly, with her sister chattering on about the upcoming encounter with Drum's family. The couple were to rendezvous at Boston's Logan Airport and rent a car for the drive to the family home. "What do you think I should wear?" Lizabeth lifted a silk dress out of her clothes bag. "What about this? It's by one of those new California designers—no, that might not go over. I'd better stick with a Chanel suit, even if it does make me feel like Jackie Kennedy circa 1960."

Steffie, obviously not comprehending her mother's references, reached out reverently to finger the silk. "It's so soft."

"Someday you'll have dresses like this, too." Lizabeth's interest in the child obviously perked up at the prospect of eventually having a stylish daughter to show off. "You won't be an outsider like I am; with Drum for a stepfather, you'll be right in the middle of things."

"I like Dave, too," the little girl ventured.

"Well, of course you do, and he's going to be your uncle!" Lizabeth winked conspiratorially at Merrie. "Oops, did I say that? Forget I mentioned it, Steffie! Now where did I pack my taupe shoes?"

And then it was time to drive to the airport through the melting snow. At the boarding gate, holding Steffie up to watch the plane take off, Merrie felt her apprehensions seep back.

She was going to have to level with Dave. How would he react? And if he agreed, could they really carry it off?

Lizabeth hadn't actually made any promises about Steffie. Then there was also the touchy issue of a long, long, long engagement, which might eventually arouse some suspicions. But there was no point in borrowing trouble.

"My mommy's beautiful, isn't she?" Steffie asked wistfully as, holding hands, the two of them descended to the car.

"She certainly is."

"You're beautiful, too, Aunt Merrie."

In the middle of the parking lot, Merrie swooped down and gave the child a hug. "So are you, Steffie." She nearly added, And if you were my little girl, I'd never send you away. But it would be wrong to criticize Lizabeth to her daughter, no matter how well deserved that criticism was.

Grandma Netta had insisted on spending some time alone with her great-granddaughter that afternoon, so, after dropping the child off at the house next door, Merrie went home to face up to what she had to do.

First, she had to dial Dave's number at work, since his home number was unlisted. She tried to sound businesslike as she worked her way through the switchboard operator and two secretaries to Dave's fluid baritone.

He sounded surprised but pleased to hear from her. After an exchange of pleasantries, Merrie got to the point. "Could we meet somewhere and talk? Something's come up about Steffie, and I need your help."

"She's not sick, is she?" His concern was immediate and genuine.

"No, thank goodness." Merrie shifted the phone, wishing her hands didn't feel so damp. "Could we have a drink or something?"

"Dinner," he said promptly. "I'll make a reservation."

"Wait a minute." Merrie thought quickly. "I don't want to go anywhere fancy—I'm not in the mood. Do you know the Cockeyed Camel?"

There was a moment's pause. "Is he one of your patients?"

She chuckled in spite of her tension. "No. Just one of my favorite places. Their fried-oyster sandwich is out of this world." That might not sound like much compared to the French cuisine Dave probably preferred, but just thinking about it whetted Merrie's appetite. "Can you meet me there?"

"Six o'clock? I'll be there."

Hanging up, she wondered if she should have suggested someplace more elegant, but decided she'd feel more comfortable on familiar ground.

And she was going to need all the support she could get.

The pub was crowded and noisy as always, with an odd medley of visitors knee-deep at the bar, wearing everything from cowboy gear to business suits. Merrie gazed along the rows of wooden tables, looking for Dave, but the only familiar face she saw was that of the saucy camel eyeing her from the mural on the back wall.

Dave arrived just as Merrie was being seated. "Sorry I'm late. That interstate fouled me up again." He swung into a chair, looking quite at home in the unpretentious environment in spite of his expensive Pierre Cardin suit. Dave had the knack of never looking out of place; perhaps it was the confident way he moved, or the boyish clump of brown hair that insisted on sticking up near the crown. Or maybe, Merrie reflected uncomfortably, she was just imagining things because of the way his eyes caught hers and his hand brushed against her wrist on the table.

"I'll be glad when they get all the road work finished," she said to break the silence. And that, she re-

flected, was as much small talk as she intended to
make. "Dave, I'd better get right down to it. Lizabeth—"

A waitress swooped toward the table. "Care for
something to drink?"

They ordered wine, then perused their menus. Several times Merrie started to speak, but Dave was obviously hungry, and she finally decided to wait until
they'd ordered. Words kept turning over and over in her
mind as she sought the perfect phrasing, just the right
light tone . . . or would it be better to emphasize Steffie's
dismal prospects?

He chose the oyster sandwich, too, with a side of
fried mushrooms for them to share. Finally, they were
free to talk.

"I don't know how to tell you this," Merrie said at
last, "but we're engaged."

Dave choked over a mouthful of wine and had to
press his napkin to his mouth to stop the coughing. "I
beg your pardon?"

"It's kind of hard to explain." Merrie didn't dare
meet his eyes. "Would it help if I told you it's for a good
cause?"

"You said something about Steffie." When she finally looked up, his expression was unreadable.

"My sister's getting married and she wants to send
her daughter to boarding school. Can you imagine? I
didn't even know they took them that young . . ." With
her hands clenched and her tongue occasionally tripping
over her words, Merrie spilled out the whole story.

Dave didn't say anything until she was finished, and
then all he murmured was, "I see."

"We'd only have to pretend for Lizabeth, and she
probably won't meet you more than once or twice,"
Merrie stumbled on. "I'm hoping that by the time we

'break up,' she'll be so pleased with how Steffie's doing that she won't want to change."

"On the other hand," Dave remarked, "had you considered that this Drummond Haymes III is also going to know about our engagement? And since he's opening a new hotel here in Nashville, it's possible that he and I will know some of the same people."

Merrie felt the blood drain from her face. "Oh."

The waitress arrived with their food. In spite of the tempting aromas, Merrie wasn't sure she could eat, but Dave dug into his meal with gusto. They munched silently for a while, and she found that the oysters did indeed taste wonderful.

"You said you nearly got engaged once before," Dave observed at last.

"It would have been a disaster." Merrie took a sip of wine. "He was Lizabeth's type, not mine: sleek and self-involved. When I found out he hated children and pets, that was the end of it."

"Were you in love with him?"

"Looking back, I can see that I wasn't, or it would have hurt more when I left," Merrie said.

"Well, I *was* in love once." Dave downed one of the mushrooms. "Right out of Harvard, I thought I was the most sophisticated young man in the world, although everyone else could see I was still wet behind the ears."

It was hard to imagine a younger Dave; he seemed so self-contained, as if he had been born at the age of thirty, Merrie reflected as she finished her sandwich.

"I met Cynthia on a vacation in Florida. She was gorgeous, sweet, and obviously found me fascinating. I fell hard. Even brought her home to meet my mother." Merrie thought she detected a hint of pain in his eyes. "Mother was very much the Southern lady, very polite. I guess Cynthia was lulled into letting down her guard;

anyway, she talked too much to one of the maids, and Mother found out."

"Found out what?" Merrie wished she could soothe away the tension from Dave's face.

"That she was five years older than she'd told me. That she'd been married twice before, which she also hadn't told me. That she'd been hanging around the beach looking for a rich husband, and someone pointed me out. That—well, what's the use in going on? You get the picture. I'd made a fool of myself. When I confronted Cynthia, she admitted everything, burst into tears, and swore she really loved me. I sent her home on the next plane." He inhaled deeply and then blinked, as if returning to the present with a start.

"So you swore never to trust another woman?" Merrie guessed.

His laugh startled her. "Hardly. It was myself I didn't trust, not for a long time."

"I guess that means no, huh?" At his quizzical look, she explained, "About pretending to be engaged to me."

"Not at all. I just thought you should know my romantic history before we become betrothed." Not giving Merrie a chance to recover from that unexpected announcement, Dave signaled to the waitress. "What'll it be? Cheesecake or carrot cake?"

"Neither," Merrie said.

"We'll share an order of cheesecake," Dave told the waitress, then turned back to Merrie and lifted his wineglass. "A toast. To our future."

Feeling dazed and off-center, Merrie clinked glasses with him and took a swallow. "You're really going to do it?"

"Isn't that what you wanted?"

"Yes, but the whole thing seems so preposterous." Finally, a sliver of light shone through the murk. He'd agreed! Steffie was safe! "Thanks, Dave. I can't tell you how much I appreciate this."

The cheesecake arrived, split onto two plates, and Merrie was glad when she tasted it that Dave hadn't followed her instructions. "What do we do next?" Her mind raced ahead. She would need a ring to wear when Lizabeth was around—no, the engagement was supposed to be a secret. Well—

"I expect my fiancée to accompany me on New Year's Eve." Dave spoke matter-of-factly. "Kip's giving a party. I realize we can't tell anyone our wonderful news, but it'll give us a chance to get into our roles."

That sounded reasonable to Merrie. "Grandma Netta usually has a few old friends over for bridge—she won't mind if Steffie is there, too."

"Fine." Dave picked up the check before Merrie could grab it. "I may be working through dinner, so I'll be at your house tomorrow around nine. The party starts at eight, but nobody gets there on time. Wear something smashing."

Before Merrie could respond, he brushed a kiss across her cheek and made his way out of the restaurant, his tall form weaving through the cluster of people waiting for tables.

He was going to do it! Merrie nibbled at the last of her cheesecake. Her crazy scheme might actually work, and no harm done.

Except—was taking her to a New Year's Eve party just an impulse, or did Dave mean to make more of this engagement than she'd intended?

As she rose to leave, an old saying popped into Merrie's head. Something about jumping out of the frying pan and into the fire.

Well, it was too late to back out now.

CHAPTER
Seven

SMASHING. THAT DIDN'T describe anything in her wardrobe, Merrie had to admit as she surveyed the contents of her closet that night and thought enviously of Lizabeth's designer silk dresses. Well, she would have to go shopping.

So, on her lunch hour Thursday, Merrie went to the mall in Green Hills and prowled restlessly through the shops. Buying fancy dresses wasn't her style, but she didn't want to let Dave down. Besides, as Grandma Netta had pointed out when they discussed the encounter, it wouldn't hurt Merrie to spruce up her image a bit.

"Sprucing up." It made her feel like a leftover Christmas tree, she thought, eyeing a tall pine sparkling with ornaments in one of the stores.

Having confined herself for so long to practical garments for veterinary work, Merrie had forgotten the thrill of trying on beautiful clothes, how sensuous they felt against the skin, how clear and fresh the colors were. Studying herself in a dressing-room mirror, she tried to imagine Dave's reaction when he came to the door tonight.

The dress she was trying on had a deeply slashed neckline, its emerald color bringing out the green glimmer in Merrie's eyes. And the way it hugged her figure left little to the imagination.

Wrong, wrong, wrong. Merrie suppressed a twinge of regret as she unzipped it. This was definitely not the sort of dress one wore to keep a relationship casual.

Three stores later, she came across a dress that met all her requirements. It, too, was emerald green—after seeing herself in that color, she simply couldn't settle for less—but it had a modestly high neckline and old-fashioned puffed sleeves. Not the latest style, but it did possess a certain flare of its own, she decided, trying not to wince at the price as she handed the saleswoman her credit card.

Steffie was delighted to see her aunt's new dress, and both she and Netta obviously were looking forward to an evening spent in each other's company. One of Netta's bridge-playing friends was bringing her young granddaughter, and Steffie couldn't wait to meet her new playmate.

So Merrie was left with a half hour to herself, to finish dressing and apply her makeup in the quiet house. Instinctively, she caught herself listening for the child's noises, and missing them.

How much more would it hurt, losing the little girl entirely?

Her thoughts returned, inevitably, to Dave. Replaying their conversation of the previous evening, Merrie felt more puzzled than ever. He'd been so matter-of-fact about everything, as if faking an engagement were an everyday occurrence. Yet she would have sensed, even without his tale of the lamentable Cynthia, that Dave was a man who took his involvements seriously.

The doorbell rang long before she was mentally prepared, even though her watch insisted it was nine o'clock. Merrie tried to descend with an air of calm deliberation, but instead scurried down the last few steps when the bell sounded again.

"Hi." She opened the door to a blast of cold air and stepped aside as Dave pressed by, his tweed coat smelling of after shave and wool. "Cold out there."

"Freezing." He stood back to survey Merrie as she snapped the door shut. "That's the perfect color for you."

"Thanks." It was ridiculous how awkward she felt, after how easily she and Dave had romped in the snow a week before. Maybe it was the way he was regarding her, with a wry tenderness that made her heart turn over. "It's kind of conservative, I guess."

"You still haven't learned to take compliments, have you?" He leaned forward before she could protest and, his cold nose touching the vulnerable hollow of her throat, inhaled her scent. "You smell nice, too."

Merrie sidled away nervously and tried to inject a light note to hide the way her breathing had speeded up. "Is that how sophisticated people talk? 'You smell nice.' What did you expect, eau de veterinarian?"

Chuckling, Dave helped her on with her coat. "I know better than to try to win you with flattery. You *do* smell nice, that's all, kind of fresh and homey. What perfume is that, anyway?"

"I'm not wearing any," she admitted, and felt her tension ebb as she laughed. With Dave, she could be herself, even if he *was* disturbingly handsome and behaving in a far more attentive manner than she would have liked. "Look, you don't have to play the smitten lover with me when we're alone, okay? Save it for Lizabeth."

"I need the practice." He turned away, reopening the door, and Merrie couldn't see his expression.

They hurried down the walk together, teeth gritted against the wind. It was a relief to settle into the gray Mercedes and feel the heat blast against her feet.

It was odd how much at home Merrie felt, riding through the night beside Dave. As if they'd known each other for much longer than a week and a half; as if they shared a lengthy past. She couldn't remember ever feeling this at ease with a man. The air seemed filled with shared thoughts and experiences even though neither of them spoke.

They arrived all too soon at Kip's low modern home, full of unexpected angles and inviting windows. Bright against the darkness, it looked even more intriguing than when Merrie had dropped Dave there on Christmas Day. "Your friend must have had this house specially designed."

"Kip fell in love with the lot and hired an architect to make the most of it." Dave halted the car in a large turnaround, behind a Porsche. "He makes good money and he knows how to enjoy it."

"Where does he keep the sleigh?" Merrie had to wait for an answer as Dave came around the car.

"In storage." He gripped Merrie's arm firmly. Just as she was about to protest, her heel slipped on a patch of ice and she careened into his side. "Careful. I don't want to take you home in an ambulance."

"I'm not used to high heels." Merrie tried not to think about how solid Dave felt, his muscular build apparent even through the heavy coat, or about how much she suddenly wished they were spending the evening alone instead of attending a party.

It was only a few steps to the front door, and after a moment their host admitted them to the warm interior, already filled with partygoers. There was hardly time to brace herself; meeting new people had never been Merrie's forte, and especially not in groups.

She hadn't gotten a good look at Kip on Christmas Eve, and would never have recognized him without his elf costume. He was tall and slender, and impeccably dressed in a silk jacket and slacks, but the thing she noticed most was the genuine delight with which he greeted Dave.

"Hey, I'm glad you made it. People have been asking about you. We've got plenty to eat and drink, and there'll be music for dancing." Kip glanced over his shoulder, apparently at someone in the next room. "Merrie, you don't mind if I let Dave introduce you around, do you? I was having a fascinating conversation with an even more fascinating blonde . . ."

"Not at all." She waved his apology aside. "You have a beautiful house."

"Thanks. We'll chat later." And he vanished, taking their coats with him.

"Kip's always falling in love with the most unattainable women," Dave said. "I hope this one isn't as self-centered as his usual choices."

"Maybe we'll get to meet her later." Merrie was glad to have a moment to collect herself and look around. The home was truly stunning. None of the rooms was conventionally laid out, and it took her a while to see how one flowed into another. Each piece of furniture was handcrafted, many with inlays and parquets; the carpeting and walls were an ivory color that set off the bright clothing of the guests as if the decor had been designed with them in mind. And perhaps, if Kip loved to entertain as much as she suspected, it had been.

In the soft, indirect lighting, she tried to sort out her impressions of the other guests. There was quite a range of ages, from early twenties on up to late sixties. Most of the women wore designer gowns; Merrie's year in New York had taught her to recognize one-of-a-kind garments, with their unique tailoring and expensive fabrics. The sleek lines made her feel a touch dowdy, and she began to wish she'd bought the more daring dress.

Dave's touch on her arm reminded her of his presence. "See anyone you know?"

"Are you kidding?" Merrie returned. "Maybe if they'd brought their pets . . ."

"You're hopeless." But he sounded amused rather than exasperated as he guided her toward the refreshment table. "How about something hot to drink? I think I smell cider."

"Perfect." But they hadn't gone more than a few steps before someone hailed Dave, and people began drifting their way. It was hard to sort them out, with so many introductions, and after a while Merrie merely smiled and nodded without trying to remember the names.

Then Dave turned, and Merrie, her hand on his arm, felt him stiffen briefly. She followed his gaze to a tall older woman standing in the doorway to the kitchen, her profile to them. Her silvering hair was upswept and her lavender dress rippled with gold threads, creating an impression of royalty.

"I wish I'd known my mother was going to be here," Dave murmured, too low for anyone else to hear. "I would have prepared you."

Merrie tried to recall what he'd said about his mother and how she'd treated Cynthia. Politely, of course; Sarah Anders was a Southern lady. But it hadn't taken her long to find out the truth about Dave's fiancée.

On the other hand, there was no reason for her to think Merrie was anything more than a casual date. And, regarding the rigidly erect figure of the elder woman, Merrie was glad of that.

"We'd better say hello." Dave was leading her forward, toward the kitchen door. "Mother?"

Sarah turned. Merrie knew instinctively that Dave's

mother had spotted them before, and taken their measure. But it was impossible to read anything but distant friendliness in those gray eyes, so like Dave's.

"I'd like you to meet a special friend of mine, Merrie McGregor." Dave kept one arm protectively encircling Merrie's waist, and to her surprise she was glad of the gesture.

Sarah Anders obviously didn't miss a thing, not the way her son was holding Merrie or the word *special* in his introduction. "I'm delighted to meet you." She hesitated only a fraction of a second. "If I'm not mistaken, your mother was Georgia Hixton, wasn't she?"

Merrie fought down the instinct to squirm like a schoolchild confronted by a stern teacher. "Yes—" She bit her tongue to stop the instinctive "ma'am" that nearly intruded. "You went to school together, I believe."

"I'm impressed," Dave said. "You two sound as if you'd been studying up on each other."

He deserved a swift kick in the ankle, but Merrie refrained, and his mother ignored the remark. "What's Georgia up to these days?"

"Well, she's married to a Frenchman and living on the Riviera." That didn't sound so bad; there was no need to point out that Georgia was now Gigi and had deducted ten years from her age.

"She was a year behind me, you know," Sarah observed. "A lovely girl. You've inherited some of her looks, my dear."

"Not as much as my sister," Merrie said, and then added, "I mean, thank you."

"Merrie has a hard time accepting compliments unless they're accompanied by barking." At his mother's blank expression, Dave added, "She's a veterinarian."

"Oh, yes, of course." Sarah Anders smiled vaguely.

"So nice to meet you. Dave, we'll be expecting you for brunch tomorrow."

"Yes, Mother." He waited until Sarah had drifted into the kitchen before explaining. "She always has friends over for brunch and to watch the football games on New Year's Day."

"She's . . . a real lady." Merrie didn't know what else to say. Sarah Anders made her feel completely inadequate, as if she'd blundered into the wrong party and everyone was trying to make the best of it. Yet Dave's mother had behaved with perfectly good manners. Now she understood how Cynthia must have felt, and sympathized in spite of Cynthia's indefensible behavior.

Other acquaintances closed in around them, and Merrie spent most of the rest of the evening listening to conversations about people and events that meant nothing to her. Dave made a valiant effort to bring the talk to more general topics, but he was swimming upstream, and after a couple of hours he pulled Merrie into a hallway where they could talk quietly.

"If it weren't so bone-chilling outside, I'd suggest we go out on the patio and look at the stars," he murmured. "But there's no way to escape. Unless we go welcome in the New Year at my place?"

The last thing Merrie would have chosen to do that evening was to spend it alone at Dave's house. It was too dangerous by far. But forcing herself to smile and look interested in subjects she didn't care about was exhausting. And Merrie had a superstition that New Year's Eves were special; they set the tone for the year to come.

"I guess we'd better," she admitted. "Not that the party isn't lovely—"

"Lovely is an adjective Southern women apply to things they ought to like but don't," Dave said, guiding her toward Kip, who was in an adjoining room, to make their farewells.

Kip was still rooted in conversation with his blonde, or at least Merrie assumed it was the same woman. She was short and buxom, with bright brown eyes, platinum-dyed hair, and a way of surveying her surroundings that gave Merrie the impression there were price tags on the furniture.

As soon as Kip looked up, Dave made a vague excuse about toasting in the New Year with Merrie's niece and grandmother. A few minutes later, they were on their way through the frosty night.

"It's a funny thing about New Year's Eve," Merrie murmured as she huddled into her coat, waiting for the car heater to warm up. "I always think back to where I was the year before."

"And where were you a year ago?" Dave kept his eyes on the road, almost empty of traffic now.

"At Bill and Sue Brown's," Merrie recalled.

"With anyone special?"

She shook her head. "Where were you last year?"

He slowed down cautiously before taking a curve. "Usually, I go to Kip's, but last year my mother and I had dinner out and then went to a movie. She dropped a few hints about young women she knew who were both suitable and unattached. I even took one of them out, but we didn't hit it off."

"I wish you were someone else." As soon as the words slipped out, Merrie wished she hadn't spoken, but it was too late to take them back. "I mean, that you didn't come from such a prominent family."

"And didn't have such an intimidating mother?" Dave glanced at her sympathetically. "Don't let her browbeat you."

"It's not that . . ." Merrie let the sentence trail away.

She didn't know how to explain that she'd spent most of her adult life fighting her mother and sister's subtle and not-so-subtle pressure to push her into a world she disliked, a socialite world that Dave couldn't avoid because of who he was. She liked some of the people she'd met, and supposed she probably could even come to like his mother, but she could never live the way they did.

On the other hand, no one had asked her to.

Dave turned off the main road onto a residential street. The houses were set back, their broad lawns silver in the moonlight.

He eased into a driveway that wound between rows of dark, bare trees. In the summer, it must be a stunning entrance, Merrie realized as they emerged into a circular turnaround before the impressive pillars of a great house that brought to mind Tara from *Gone with the Wind*.

"Not exactly what I expected," Merrie admitted.

A flicker of surprise crossed Dave's face. "You don't like it? It's a bit formal, I guess, but I had to plan for the future. It's too cold to sit here and talk; let's go inside."

The interior was just as elegant as the outside. The hand of a designer was evident in the blend of antique furniture with newer pieces, in the formal draperies looped across the vast front windows, in the paintings of English hunting scenes.

At least the heating system worked, she mused as Dave led the way to the kitchen, where, after disposing of their coats, he began making coffee.

The country-style kitchen was also large, but it had a homey feel, and from where she sat at the breakfast table, Merrie could see an adjacent den stuffed with books and magazines. A newspaper had been left open on the foot of a recliner, with a crocheted comforter tossed over the back. This, she gathered, was where Dave really lived.

"Do you actually need such a big place?" she ventured.

"Not at the moment." He fetched mugs for the coffee. "Once a year, just before Thanksgiving, I host all my management personnel and their husbands and wives; it's a family tradition. That's when we open up the house, bring in the caterers and so on, now that my mother prefers to live in a condominium close to her friends."

"Oh." Finally, Merrie thought she understood. "This was your parents' home?"

Dave shook his head. "No. That had too many memories. I needed a place that was really mine. I always felt a bit like an adolescent in their house."

So this was how Dave intended to live, in a manor, so to speak. What sort of woman would live here with him? Merrie wondered. An old friend his mother would approve of? Or someone like Lizabeth, who hadn't been born to wealth but would relish presiding over such formal surroundings?

Definitely not someone like Merrie, who preferred a touch of chaos and a house where children and animals could romp freely. Which reminded her of something. "Where's Buster?"

"Asleep on our coats." Dave carried the steaming cups to the table. "I didn't think you'd mind."

"Of course not." Merrie stared down at the oak surface of the kitchen table. "Isn't this a little impractical?"

Dave followed her glance. "That's why I have placemats."

"Yes, but children—" Merrie stopped herself. "I'm sorry. You'd think I was buying the thing, wouldn't you?"

He rested his elbows comfortably on the table. "There's a smaller kitchen upstairs—practically bullet-proof, the decorator assured me. This one's geared more toward caterers, although I kind of like it. Eating upstairs makes me feel like I'm in exile."

And how do you think a child would feel? Not wanting to broach a subject that was none of her business, Merrie searched for a neutral topic of conversation. "How did you choose your decorator?"

"She's the same one my mother used. I like the classic look. Hey, I nearly forgot." Dave paced over to the cupboard and pulled out a box of doughnuts. "Let's pig out."

Tension bubbled away from Merrie and she giggled at the image of Dave, dressed in an elegant suit, licking doughnut glaze from his fingers.

"You already know they're one of my weaknesses," she accused, examining the contents and selecting one.

"I've still got to find out what the other ones are." He settled next to her, his hand brushing her wrist as he reached for a second doughnut. The touch tingled up to Merrie's shoulder and down her side. "So I can play on them shamelessly."

"You already are. Doughnuts and coffee. It's sheer heaven," she admitted.

"Not quite." He leaned toward Merrie and closed his mouth over hers. Since she'd just bitten off a section of doughnut, the sensation was novel and enticing: an almost indecently intimate fullness, coupled with the sweetness of the doughnut and the slight roughness of Dave's kiss.

"Mmm." He lifted his head and gazed down at her. "I think I've found another weakness."

"You just invented that one." She knew she ought to

move away, but she couldn't. If he was going to kiss her again, she didn't want to miss it.

This time, there was no doughnut to intervene. A hint of teeth, the flick of his tongue, and the gentle grip of his hands on Merrie's shoulders carried her out of herself, into a realm of pleasurable yielding. She nestled closer, lifting her hand to touch Dave's neck and scarcely noticing the crumbs she dropped onto his collar.

"There's one thing I definitely don't like about kitchens." Without giving her time to object, Dave lifted Merrie to her feet and guided her into the den. "They were designed for cooking and eating, heaven knows why, when there are much more interesting things to do."

He scooped her onto the recliner and squeezed in beside her, knocking a section of newspaper to the floor. From across the room came the soft thump of Buster's tail from a loveseat where the collie was, indeed, lying on their coats.

"Dave . . ." Merrie's token effort at protest died as Dave's strong arms clasped her, and his mouth claimed hers with deep hunger. An answering need welled up in Merrie, and she responded with a passion that was new to her, a calling from one carefully guarded heart to another. His lips on hers, the whisper of his eyelashes against her brow, his fingers savoring the softness of her cheek, became a bond between them.

His arousing nearness wiped away her caution as Merrie's tongue tasted the corners of his mouth. Warm breath sighed across her neck, and he found the inviting pulse of her throat, barely revealed by the high-collared dress. Then he loosened the dress and his tongue licked down over her collarbones, raising fire in its wake.

Who was this woman, this other Merrie who wanted

to be possessed and raised to ecstasy? Had he created her, or only discovered a long-dormant part of Meredith McGregor? For a moment, she didn't care. She simply wanted this closeness to spiral and peak, to surge and lift her into new realms. She wanted everything, no matter what the cost.

How sturdy and firm Dave felt in her arms. She could lean on him and lose herself in him, and never look back. This was how it felt to surrender to a man, to forget herself and know that she would be taken care of, safe within his protective arms . . .

Had she gone mad?

The unwelcome thought trembled on the edge of Merrie's awareness. She tried to push it away, but it hovered there, facing her down.

There was no such thing as losing yourself in another person. The morning would come, bringing its clear revealing light, and you had to get up and deal with your own life again.

She needed a man, yes. A man very much like Dave. She wished it could be him, but it couldn't. *He's right. He does play on my weaknesses shamelessly. And I can't let him.*

She knew instinctively that if she allowed it, Dave would overwhelm her. Not only physically, but in every way. Through the doorway, Merrie's gaze took in the grand kitchen and, visible beyond it, a formal dining room. Chandeliers and antique tables. A house for entertaining; a house for someone like Lizabeth, or Sarah Anders. Not for Merrie.

The worst of it was that a part of her, conditioned by her mother and sister, still longed to be pampered and petted and wear designer dresses and be the envy of other women. That was the part of herself Dave appealed to most, and it was also the part of herself she liked least.

Beside her, Dave lay still, obviously aware of her change in mood. "Are we going too fast?" His quiet tone calmed her thoughts.

"I'm sorry." Awkwardly, Merrie sat up and refastened the back of her dress. "I shouldn't have let things get this far."

"We're both grown-ups." Dave watched her from where he reclined. "What's wrong, Merrie?"

"Everything." She stood up, trying to find the right words and failing. "Dave, I can't explain myself. You could argue with me and you'd be right, but we can't go on seeing each other."

"That's the most ridiculous thing I ever heard." Anger edged his voice as he swung up to confront her. "Merrie, if you had the idea that I was pressuring you—"

"No, it isn't that. I was a willing partner." She lifted her hand, as if to stop his advance. "It's me. I can't handle this relationship right now, and I'm sorry if that sounds adolescent. I'll understand if you don't want to continue with the mock engagement—"

"And let your sister stick Steffie in some damn boarding school?" He scowled. "Look, we need to talk about this when we're both feeling more rational. I'm tied up tomorrow during the day, but I want us to have dinner. Alone."

"No." Crossing the room, Merrie retrieved her coat from beneath the dozing collie. "Dave, please. Can we just do this my way? When I need you to help persuade Lizabeth, I'll give you a call. Okay?"

"And when will that be?" Angrily, he shrugged on his own coat.

"Fairly soon, I expect." An image of Lizabeth, eager

for her upcoming wedding, popped into Merrie's mind. "Since her fiancé had business in Nashville, I imagine they'll come to town before long. Besides, she's got to pick up Steffie sometime, and if my sister thinks I'm going to put that little girl on a plane to New York by herself, she'd better think again."

For the first time since Merrie had withdrawn, Dave's expression softened. "You look so fierce, like a mama bear protecting her cub."

"That's how I feel." Merrie hesitated in the doorway to the kitchen. "Dave . . ." Oh, damn, what *did* she want to say, anyway? "Thanks for helping. With Steffie, I mean."

"I make no promises about keeping away from you." Reluctantly, he followed her out of the den. "As it happens, I've let a lot of work slide over the holidays, and I've got to make some trips out of town over the next few weeks. But then—"

"We'll deal with 'then' when it comes." Merrie helped herself to another doughnut on her way out of the house.

"Don't forget," he said as their footsteps crunched over the thin remaining crust of snow. "I know your weaknesses."

"Not all of them." Somewhere a firecracker sounded, followed by the tootling of paper horns, and shouts echoed faintly from a neighboring house. "Happy New Year, Dave." Merrie didn't dare look into his eyes.

"Yes, it will be—happier than you think."

She couldn't decide whether his words sounded more like a threat or a promise.

CHAPTER
Eight

"Ow!" THE RACQUETBALL grazed the side of Merrie's head as it whizzed by, and she stumbled backward. The weariness of a long day at the clinic and the strain of competing full steam on the court combined to buckle her knees and land her unceremoniously on her backside, her racquet clattering down beside her.

"Are you all right?" Sue Brown dropped her own racquet and knelt at Merrie's side, gently examining the spot where the ball had hit. "Those things are dangerous."

"You're the nurse. You tell me—am I going to make it?" Merrie tried to laugh but winced instead.

"Looks like it just grazed the scalp." Sue helped her to her feet. "Let's call it a day, shall we?"

"Sounds good to me." Letting her friend bring the racquets, Merrie trudged out, past a couple who were waiting to use the court, and down the hall to the health club's locker room.

A few minutes later, freshly showered and changed into street clothes, the two women emerged into the early evening darkness. The air chilled Merrie's nose and cheeks, but at least the ground was clear of snow.

"Are you sure you're going to be okay?" Sue studied Merrie closely. "You seem a little unsteady on your feet."

"Just tired." Merrie's head was beginning to throb,

but she didn't feel like being fussed over, and she certainly didn't want to be dragged off to some doctor's office. As Sue had said, it was only a graze. "What I need is dinner."

"It's not like you to get hit like that." Sue wasn't easily dissuaded. "You've been distracted the last couple of weeks. If I didn't know better, I'd say you had man trouble."

Sue was being much too perceptive. "I'll see you next week, okay?" Merrie made a show of striding firmly to her car, but the minute Sue turned away, she winced and let her shoulders sag.

Man trouble. Absence-of-man trouble was more like it, Merrie reflected as she started the engine. Dave had certainly taken her at her word. There'd been no contact between them in the two weeks since New Year's Eve. That was what she'd asked for, but the reality of not seeing him was a lot more painful than she'd expected.

It wasn't just that Steffie asked after him, or that Netta regarded Merrie with a concerned frown when she thought no one was looking. The problem was Merrie herself. Taking down her Christmas tree, buying doughnuts for Steffie, watching the snowman melt—little acts like that brought Dave back, so sharp-edged and real she could almost touch him. Damn the man. He'd agreed to stay out of her life, hadn't he? Then why didn't he stay out of her thoughts?

Even Merrie had to smile at the unfairness of her anger. Dave could hardly control the role he played in her imagination!

"Hi, Aunt Merrie!" Steffie dashed across the lawn from Netta's house as Merrie pulled into her driveway. For a moment, Merrie thought her niece was wearing a ginger-colored fur stole, and then she realized that Snoozer was draped around the child's shoulders. Despite his natural lethargy, he'd never allowed Merrie such familiarities.

"Well, well. That looks warm." She bent down to give Steffie a kiss. "What have you been up to?"

"Gramma Netta and I fed the birds, and I had to keep chasing Wanderer away, so we fed the cats, too." The words tumbled over each other as Steffie trailed along. "Oh, and Mommy called, and she said you should call her."

Merrie's head began to ache again as she unlocked her door. "Did she say why?"

"No. What're we having for dinner?"

"Chili." Merrie was grateful that she'd prepared food ahead of time; right now, she could barely think, let alone plan a meal.

Steffie ploughed zestfully through two bowls of chili and three biscuits. The weekend lay ahead, and she was having a sleepover Saturday night with the little girl she'd made friends with on New Year's Eve. "Maybe I'll take Snoozer. Don't you think she'd like that?"

"Maybe, but I doubt if her mother would." Merrie picked distractedly at her chili. What did Lizabeth want? Had she changed her mind about letting Steffie stay in Nashville? Had a wedding date been set?

Merrie delayed calling until Steffie was bathed and tucked into bed. She just didn't feel up to putting on a happy face for the child if the news was bad.

Finally, there was no more reason to procrastinate. Reluctantly, Merrie picked up the phone and tapped out her sister's number.

Lizabeth answered on the second ring, her voice so cheerful Merrie half-expected her to burst into song.

"Well, don't keep me in suspense," Merrie said. "What's up?"

"Lots and lots!" It was easy to visualize Lizabeth

stretching her long legs across the cream-colored sofa in her vast living room, her delicate fingers entwined around the stem of a wine glass. "First of all, Boston."

"That's right; how was his family?" Merrie had purposely called from the kitchen, where it wouldn't matter if she nervously spilled some of her decaf, but instead she found herself sipping it with a semblance of calm. If there was a bomb to be dropped, Lizabeth was obviously not ready to detonate it yet.

For the next quarter of an hour, her sister described in juicy detail the mansion, Rolls Royce, and impeccable dress of the Haymeses of Boston—where they had taken her, to whom they had introduced her, and what they had eaten.

"They were lovely, really," she concluded. "Not particularly warm, of course, but they extended every courtesy. I gathered they were relieved to find I wasn't some tramp with bleached hair and too much makeup. Can you imagine? I mean, Drum is the soul of discretion. He'd never go out with anyone like that, but I suppose if *I* were his mother, I'd worry, too."

The fact that Lizabeth was actually able to project herself into Mrs. Haymes' perspective was a good sign, Merrie reflected as she stretched the phone cord to its limit so she could heat up some more decaf in the microwave. It might even indicate a newfound touch of maturity on her sister's part.

Then, just as Merrie was beginning to conclude there was no reason for concern, Lizabeth said, "Oh, I knew there was something else I meant to tell you. Drum and I are coming to Nashville tomorrow."

Merrie sputtered as a mouthful of coffee went down the wrong way. "Tomorrow?"

"I meant to call you earlier in the week, but things have been hectic." She could visualize Lizabeth waving an arm airily, as if casually dismissing the rudeness of giving someone only a few hours' notice about such a visit. So much for newfound maturity.

"Do—do you need a place to stay?" Merrie blurted without thinking.

"Don't be silly." Lizabeth's warm chuckle coated the telephone line all the way from New York. "Most of the rooms are already finished at Drum's hotel. In fact, that's why we're coming; he wants to review the plans for the opening."

"So you'll be staying quite awhile?" Merrie probed.

"Oh, a few days. Who knows?" Lizabeth obviously was no longer concerned about returning for modeling bookings in New York, but then, why should she be? "Anyway, isn't it lovely? We'll have a chance to meet your fiancé, and of course I do miss Steffie so much. You know, I'm just not sure what to do about her schooling. She *is* my daughter now, and I want the best for her."

"So do I." Hearing the grim note in her voice, Merrie added quickly, "I'm not sure if Dave will be able to make it; he said something about going out of town."

"Oh, we can stay long enough to meet him." Lizabeth proceeded to give Merrie her flight number and time of arrival. "Of course, we can have someone from the hotel pick us up."

"No, I'll be there." It was a relief when the conversation finally ended, and Merrie hung up the phone.

Was it only the racquetball accident that made her brain buzz? she wondered as she sat in the kitchen contemplating the merits of absconding with Steffie to a desert island.

There was simply no help for it. She was going to have to call Dave. With a sigh, Merrie reached for her address holder and flipped it to *A*. His phone number, newly inscribed, leaped up at her, and she dialed it quickly before she lost her nerve.

At the sound of Dave's rich-timbred "Hello," nervous excitement tingled through Merrie. His next words stopped her. "Sorry I'm not home to take your call . . ."

Whoever invented answering machines must have been a sadist. Her next thought was: If Dave's not home on a Friday night, where is he?

Perhaps out of town. Or on a date? He had every right, but Merrie felt a flare of something that might have been jealousy.

The beep of the answering machine cut off her musings, and she realized she hadn't prepared what to say. "This is Merrie." Now, there was a brilliant opening. "Lizabeth just called to say she and Drum are coming to town tomorrow—that's Saturday. Is this one of those thirty-second messages or can I talk longer?" She felt like a fool, asking a machine a question. "I mean, they'd like to meet you. Can we arrange something? Do you really listen to these recordings or do they self-destruct after ten minutes? 'Bye."

Somebody ought to teach classes in how to talk to answering machines, Merrie reflected as she hung up.

She marched up to bed, still trying to identify the stomach-hanging-in-the-air sensation that had plagued her ever since Lizabeth's call.

Finally, she placed it. It was the same feeling she'd gotten once when she let someone talk her into riding on a roller coaster, just as it topped the highest slope and paused for an instant before the crazy, terrifying, mind-numbing swoop downhill.

"Merrie!" Lizabeth, elegant in a chignon and Chanel suit, darted through the arriving passengers, towing a startled man behind her. From his clipped, silvering hair to his expensively shod feet, Drummond Haymes III was the picture of a conservative businessman in his late forties. His saving grace was an unruly set of eyebrows that looked as if they ought to belong to a mad scientist.

Introductions and kisses-into-the-air were traded all around. Steffie alternated jumping eagerly with clinging to Merrie's hand in sudden fits of shyness.

Despite her sister's almost overwhelming presence, Merrie tried to focus on Drum and his response to Steffie. He gave the girl a long if rather stiff hug—nothing objectionable there—but other than that took little notice of her.

In the car, he didn't seem to begrudge Steffie's request to sit beside her mother, but mostly he plied Merrie with questions about Nashville's building boom. There was no antagonism between the prospective stepfather and Steffie, but no particular warmth, either, Merrie concluded sadly. Or perhaps Drum simply wasn't a demonstrative person. She decided it was only fair to reserve judgment.

"I left a message on Dave's machine, but apparently he's out of town," she said as they reached the hotel. Their plan was to drop off Drum's and Lizabeth's luggage, then head to Merrie's house for lunch. Netta was attending a bridge club meeting and would join them later.

"I'm looking forward to meeting this fiancé of yours," Drum said as he helped Lizabeth out of the car. "I hear he's in business?"

Merrie opened her mouth to explain, but just then a staff member showed up, showering effusions over Drum and Lizabeth.

Drum handled the luggage with cool efficiency. Watching him in action, Merrie had the impression he disliked wasting time or energy. She could understand why he wouldn't be terribly comfortable around children.

Later, when her guests had settled back into the station wagon, Merrie found herself chattering too much as she drove, even pointing out some of Nashville's less-than-stellar sights, such as the Vanderbilt University gym. It was important for Steffie's sake to make a good impression on Drum, but Merrie had a feeling her modest, well-lived-in home wasn't likely to accomplish that.

At least the Christmas tree was gone, Merrie reflected as she showed them into the house. Last year, she hadn't gotten around to stripping off the ornaments until February.

"I thought you might enjoy some soup, in this cold weather," Merrie said as she finished hanging up the coats. "It should be nearly ready."

She stepped into the kitchen and checked the slow-cooker. Sure enough, the fragrant soup, thick with meat and vegetables, looked ready to serve.

"Smells wonderful." Drum followed her into the room, with Lizabeth and Steffie trailing behind. "You make your own soup? Impressive."

"I'm amazed," Lizabeth confessed. "Merrie usually burns everything."

"Oh, I'm improving with age." Merrie resisted the urge to give her sister a kick in the shin, and instead, busied herself tasting the soup to be sure she hadn't left anything out.

It was flat. Darn it, she'd forgotten the salt. "Are you on a low-salt diet?" she asked Drum hopefully.

"Are you kidding?" Lizabeth shot back. "This guy practically lives on pretzels. The saltier the better."

"Then I'll add some." Merrie hefted her old-fashioned pewter saltceller. "A couple of good shakes ought to do it—"

With a heart-wrenching plop, the lid fell into the pot, followed by a rush of salt. Frantically, Merrie tried to scoop out the salt with a spoon, but it sank untraceably into the liquid.

"I don't believe you did that," Lizabeth said. "On second thought, I'm not surprised."

"Blow it out your ear!" Merrie snapped, and then wanted to bite her tongue. "I didn't mean that."

"Yes, you did." Drum smiled, and for the first time she actually liked him. "I'd call that extreme provocation. What do you say we go out for lunch?"

"I could cook a potato in here," Merrie muttered, peering into the soup. "It's supposed to absorb the salt."

"Let's go to McDonald's!" Steffie piped up. Drum winced.

"Let's not," Lizabeth said.

The sound of the doorbell was a welcome relief, even if it probably would only turn out to be somebody selling cemetery plots or cosmetics. Wiping her hands on a kitchen towel, Merrie headed for the front door.

She was greeted, upon opening the door, by the sight of a puppy with matted fur and lively eyes, wriggling in the gentle grasp of a mud-covered figure that bore a curious resemblance to Dave Anders. At least, it was the same height and had gray eyes; beyond that, it was difficult to tell much.

"Sorry for all the mud." He remained standing on the step. "He got away from me."

It was possible, Merrie considered, that she had just stepped through the looking glass into an alternate reality. Or perhaps someone had spiked the soup and she was hallucinating. On the other hand, maybe Dave Anders really was standing here caked with mud, offering her a dirty puppy that, on closer inspection, appeared to be a collie.

"Oh, look!" Steffie raced up. "Is that for me? Can I have it?"

"Don't touch that thing!" Lizabeth loomed in the doorway. "Steffie, come here this minute!"

Dave took in the situation with a look of mingled embarrassment and guilt. "I guess I should have listened to my answering machine, huh?"

Merrie inhaled deeply, but it didn't dispel the grubby image in front of her, so she decided to make the best of things. "Dave, I'd like you to meet my sister Lizabeth and her husband-to-be, Drum Haymes." She didn't dare turn around yet to see their reaction. "Folks, somewhere underneath all this mud is Dave Anders, my"—she nearly choked on the word—"fiancé."

A glance at Drum showed her the worst: He was trying to be polite, but his nostrils flared with distaste. If it were possible to create a worse first impression, she couldn't imagine how.

"There really is a reasonable explanation for this," Dave said. "Mind if I clean up a bit first?"

"We'd be grateful." Lizabeth led Steffie away to the living room.

While Merrie settled the puppy in the utility room, Dave went back to his car and returned with a suitcase. "I always keep a bag packed," he explained as he headed for the bathroom.

At least Drum ought to appreciate the efficiency of that approach, Merrie thought, but she could tell from the way her guests were sitting stiffly in the living room that they weren't exactly overwhelmed with warm feelings.

To further complicate matters, Steffie disobeyed her mother by dashing into the utility room to play with the puppy, which was touching noses with a distinctly wary Snoozer. Homebody and Wanderer darted out of sight as

Merrie dusted off the little girl and returned her to the front room.

Dave emerged with his hair wet and slicked back, but otherwise looking impressively businesslike in his expensive suit. "First, let me apologize for the intrusion." Without asking her permission, he walked over to the liquor cabinet. "Second, let me pour you folks a drink. What'll it be?"

He certainly was acting as if he belonged here, Merrie noted, not sure whether to be grateful or annoyed as he poured scotch for Drum and amaretto for Lizabeth, adding a soda pop for Steffie. Merrie declined a drink, not wanting to risk even the least sign of tipsiness. She'd gotten into enough trouble so far this morning without any help.

"Now for the explanation." Dave stood beside Merrie's chair. She couldn't see him, not without turning and craning her neck, but his nearness enveloped her: the masculine scent touched with earthiness, the warmth and solidity of his body, the powerful rumble of his voice. She was surprised to feel her muscles starting to relax. *Maybe he really can pull out of this one. Who could resist him?*

"I happen to own a champion collie, as Merrie knows." Dave took a sip of his Perrier before continuing. "As a favor to a friend, I arranged for Buster to sire some purebred puppies."

Even Lizabeth looked mildly impressed. "They must be worth quite a bit."

"Yes, and they're beautiful animals." Dave managed to sound as if he were chatting easily with old friends. "I got back from a trip late last night and unfortunately didn't bother to listen to my messages. This morning, I dropped by to see the puppies."

"I hope you weren't bringing that one for Steffie."

Drum shot a stern look at the little girl, who was squirming in her mother's arms at the sound of puppy toenails on the utility-room floor.

"Not exactly." That meant yes-but-I-didn't-know-you'd-be-here, Merrie translated mentally, grateful for Dave's willingness to prevaricate on her behalf. "When I arrived, they informed me that one of the puppies was deaf and would have to be destroyed."

"How cruel!" Lizabeth looked horrified. "That's no reason to kill an animal! Not that I particularly like dogs, but what does a dog need to hear for, anyway? It's not as if they talk on the telephone!"

"If the trait is genetic, no one would want a defect like that continuing in a line of purebred animals," Dave pointed out. "But it may be just an accident. Besides, if the puppy is raised as a pet and not bred, what's the difference? So I brought him over here for Merrie to take a look at, to be sure there aren't any other problems with him."

"I want to keep him!" Steffie's eyes flashed with a passion Merrie had never seen before. "His name is Puddles, and he's mine!"

"Puddles?" Drum shook his head. "Lizabeth, please explain to her that it's impossible."

"Why don't we eat first?" As she spoke, Merrie's ears picked up the sound of Netta's car outside. "Maybe our grandmother can give Steffie some lunch and help her bathe Puddles, while we indulge in some adult conversation." Without waiting for a reply, she dashed outside.

The next few minutes passed in a haze. Grandma Netta immediately sized up the situation and volunteered to baby-sit, and in no time Drum and Lizabeth were safely tucked into the back of Dave's Mercedes, looking suitably placated by the expensive car.

"If you don't mind, I'd like to take you to one of my favorite restaurants." Dave pulled smoothly away from the curb. "It's in the Opryland Hotel."

"Perfect." Drum nodded appreciatively. "That's one of the places I wanted to see while I'm here."

"You like country music?" Merrie asked in surprise.

"Not the Opry. The Opryland Hotel," Lizabeth informed her with a touch of condescension. "The competition."

"Oh." Merrie sank back in her seat and determinedly kept her mouth shut for the rest of the ride, as the two men discussed business. At least, she noted with relief, Drum seemed to appreciate Dave's business acumen. Already, the negative first impression seemed to be dissipating. Thank goodness.

Once they arrived, Merrie sensed Drum taking mental notes as they entered the huge, glass-domed interior courtyard known as the Conservatory. She'd never been inside before, and couldn't help being charmed. True to its name, the Conservatory was filled with trees, plants, and fountains, just like a botanical garden. Looking up, Merrie noted five stories of hotel rooms, each with a balcony enclosed in black wrought-iron railing, New Orleans style.

"Here we are." Dave escorted them along a walkway to Rhett's, a café with tables set "outside," in the Conservatory. A waiter pulled out chairs for Lizabeth and Merrie, and she was pleased to see Drum's look of approval as he took in the napkins formally fanned above the wineglasses, and the fountain tinkling softly to the side.

"Very nice." He lifted his menu. "The most successful hotels never forget the importance of atmosphere."

"That's a delicate line in your business, isn't it?" Dave remarked. "You want a certain uniformity, so that the businessman always feels at home, and yet you want to capture a touch of the local color as well."

"Exactly." Drum perused the menu rapidly. "And speaking of local color, I think I'll try the Confederate lobster."

A glance told Merrie the lobster was served with pasta shells and tomato-lobster sauce. Quite a bit to eat for lunch—too much for her. Instead, she chose the Gulf Coast Combo, two avocado halves stuffed with seafood, while Lizabeth decided on the Key West Seafood Delight, and Dave picked the California Smoked Salmon Sandwich.

After the waiter took their orders, Drum began asking about Dave's business. As the men talked, Merrie breathed a silent prayer. *Please let him be so fascinated that he forgets about this morning. Please let them leave Steffie with me.*

It did indeed seem as if the earlier bad impression had been erased. The clink of expensive glasses, the arrival of the appetizers Dave had selected, and the murmur of voices from nearby conversations created a lulling symphony.

The other guests were well dressed, and Lizabeth was clearly looking them over. The women, Merrie guessed, wore styles much like those in New York, but perhaps with a touch more softness.

"Do you know, I've never felt comfortable in hats, but that lady over there looks splendid in one." Lizabeth gestured across the room. "Isn't she grand? Like Queen Elizabeth."

Merrie followed her gaze to a group of older women dining regally in one corner. The lady in question was turned away, listening to one of her companions. All Merrie could see was the discreet brim of her hat, the back of a tailored silk jacket, and a wisp of silvering hair at the nape.

Then the woman turned in profile, and Merrie had to stifle a gasp. With her foot, she nudged Dave lightly.

She didn't dare look at him, but she felt him turn, and he broke off in mid-sentence.

"Someone you know?" Drum asked as the older woman glanced their way.

"Yes, as a matter of fact. It's my mother." Dave stood up as he caught Sarah Anders's eye. Time seemed to slow down and the background noises to whisper away as Merrie watched Dave's mother excuse herself and start in their direction.

Maybe it would be all right, she told herself, ignoring the clenched dryness of her throat. A few introductions, a bit of chitchat . . .

She had reckoned without Lizabeth.

Her sister's first words to Sarah Anders were, "How delightful to meet you. I'm so glad your son is marrying into our family!"

CHAPTER
Nine

"I BEG YOUR PARDON?" Sarah's well-bred expression gave way to open astonishment.

"Oh, I'm sorry, I should have introduced myself." The men were already standing, and Lizabeth looked as if she weren't quite sure whether she should join them, out of respect for this clearly eminent personage. Instead, however, she extended a hand and said, "I'm Merrie's sister, Lizabeth."

"Pleased to meet you." Sarah Anders was clearly operating on automatic pilot, a lifetime pattern of correct behavior carrying her through the confusion.

Merrie didn't dare look at Dave as he completed the introductions. She'd gotten him into this mess; she only hoped his mother would understand when he explained.

"Won't you join us?" Dave offered his chair.

"Oh, please do!" cried Lizabeth as Merrie winced, wishing she could disappear through the floor.

"I'm afraid my friends would take it amiss." There was no avoiding Sarah's direct gaze as she turned to Merrie. "My dear, I'm so happy for you."

As she thanked Dave's mother, the phrase echoed in Merrie's ears. *I'm so happy for you.* What a polite, correct, thoroughly noncommittal thing to say.

So she wasn't prepared for Sarah's next statement. "If you haven't already made plans, I'd like to give the engagement party. Valentine's Day would be an appropriate occasion, I should think. Dave wouldn't mind if we used his house for the occasion, would you, dear?"

Please, let Nashville disappear beneath a volcanic eruption. Anything, anything to get me out of this.

Instead, piling shock upon shock, Dave was saying calmly, "What a generous offer, Mother. I wouldn't mind at all. Drum, Lizabeth, consider yourselves the first to be invited."

It wasn't until Sarah's figure had retreated out of earshot that Lizabeth demanded, "You mean she didn't *know?*"

"How could she?" Merrie didn't bother to hide an edge of irritation. "It was supposed to be a secret, remember?"

"Oh, that's right!" Lizabeth smacked her palm dramatically against her forehead. "How stupid of me! Merrie, Dave, do forgive me."

"Nothing to forgive. She had to find out sometime." Dave's pronouncement was startling, but before Merrie could check to see if he'd taken complete leave of his senses, the waiter arrived with their food.

She hardly tasted the meal, keenly aware that Sarah Anders was studying her from across the patio. Well, at least Merrie didn't have any scandals in her background like the long-ago Cynthia.

By tonight, Dave would no doubt have explained everything to his mother. But Sarah Anders was probably already issuing invitations and spreading the news to the ladies at her table. The upshot was going to be horribly embarrassing, and Merrie shivered in spite of the warm Conservatory air.

She was roused back to the conversation as they finished the meal. "Would you like to see my house?" Dave was asking their guests. "Or perhaps you'd rather leave that for later in your visit."

"We'd better see it now if we're going to," Drum told him. "As it turns out, I'm afraid I've got to be back in New York on Monday, which means we're flying out tomorrow night."

That, at least, was a relief, Merrie reflected as they strolled toward the car—until Lizabeth added, "I hope Steffie hasn't already set her heart on having that puppy. Of course, we can't take it back with us."

Trying not to show her dismay, Merrie said, "Steffie's welcome to stay with me as long as you like."

"That's sweet of you, but she belongs with me, after all." Lizabeth conveniently ignored the fact that she'd abandoned her child for Christmas and for two weeks afterward. "But we'll be back in a month, for your party. How exciting! I'll have to get a new gown; your future mother-in-law has that thoroughbred look I so admire. I want to choose something that's just right."

There wasn't going to be any engagement party— but what excuse would Merrie give when the event was called off? Maybe it was time to stop this charade and tell the truth. But Lizabeth would only see the whole thing as further proof of Merrie's irresponsibility. What a mess!

And why on earth had Dave given his mother permission to sponsor the party? Couldn't he have stalled until they could speak privately?

For the rest of the afternoon, Merrie puzzled over his behavior. Dave seemed to delight in playing the affable host, showing Drum and Lizabeth around his house— and plying them with drinks and amusing stories.

Not until Drum and her sister had been dropped off at their hotel did Merrie have a chance to speak to Dave alone.

Staring out the window of the Mercedes, she took a deep breath and plunged in. "Dave, why did you—"

"Your sister's very attractive. And the perfect companion for a businessman like Drum. But a mother? I can't imagine why she adopted Steffie." Dave paused at the light, tapping his fingers impatiently on the steering wheel.

Merrie shrugged. "Well, she did, that's all. And speaking of mothers—"

"Yes, speaking of *my* mother, I was surprised at her offer to sponsor a party, I have to admit." He started forward as the light turned green. "She's certainly being gracious about the whole thing."

"That's just the point—"

This time, he interrupted by saying, "I suppose she's anxious for grandchildren. She'd almost given up on ever marrying me off." Merrie couldn't seem to complete a sentence today. Was Dave cutting her off on purpose?

"Dave, why did you let her do it?" There, she'd finally gotten to the point! "Can you imagine how humiliated she'll be when she has to cancel it? She's probably invited all her friends by now!"

"I have no intention of canceling it." Dave braked to avoid a stray cat, then resumed their drive toward Merrie's house.

"Have you completely flipped out?" Merrie abandoned all attempt to stay calm. "Dave—"

"Let's not forget what's at stake here." Dave met her gaze, but his eyes were opaque. "How would it look to Lizabeth if we refused to have an engagement party? You wanted to fool her, and you have."

"But what about your mother? I didn't intend to fool *her!*"

"My mother loves children. She'd understand." That wasn't an answer and surely he knew it, but just then they arrived at Merrie's house, and Steffie came running toward them with Netta trailing behind.

Merrie's dismay over the encounter with Sarah gave way to another concern: the need to tell Steffie she was going back to New York tomorrow.

The little girl didn't take the news well.

"Do I have to?" she asked when Merrie told her, inside the warm kitchen where a freshly scrubbed Puddles was dashing from one person to another, sniffing each in turn. "Can I take him with me?"

"Yes, you have to, and no, you can't." Merrie appealed silently to Dave.

"Puddles has to stay here." He squatted down and ruffled the puppy's ears. "You can see how happy he is. Besides, you'll be coming back in a month."

"Lizabeth certainly is spending a lot of time in Nashville," Netta said. "She's already planning another visit?"

"She's coming back for our engagement party." Dave, fondling the puppy, didn't catch Netta's startled expression, but Merrie did.

"Well, it's not really an engagement party," Merrie tried to explain. "Lizabeth just thinks it is."

"Aren't you two carrying this a bit far?" Netta asked.

"I'm not going!" Steffie stamped one foot on the floor. "I'm staying here with you and Puddles. Mommy's going to leave me with a sitter all the time anyway."

Merrie gave the child a big hug. "I wish you could stay here, too, sweetie, but you can't."

The little girl continued to protest, argue, reason, and plead all the way through supper. There was no further chance to talk to Dave, who slipped away after heartily enjoying the soup—desalted with a potato. Lizabeth was the one who should have been here, reassuring her daughter, Merrie reflected as she finally tucked Steffie into bed and went downstairs. Lizabeth and Steffie would probably have a good time together when the child was older, but right now Steffie needed someone patient and nurturing. And Lizabeth wasn't showing any sign of suddenly developing those qualities.

Netta had waited up for her. "Now what's this about an engagement party?" She listened quietly to the explanation, her mouth quirking as if trying to suppress a smile.

"What do you think?" Merrie demanded when she'd finished. "We can't go through with it, can we?"

"It looks like Dave intends to." Netta took a sip of hot chocolate. "It's almost worth it, just to flush Georgia—excuse me, Gigi—out of her lovenest in France. I wish I weren't afraid of flying, but I am, and my daughter hasn't been here to visit in, what, almost two years?"

"Maybe she won't come," Merrie said hopefully, trying to imagine Sarah Anders's reaction to Gigi's somewhat flamboyant manners. "But, Netta, by the time we get around to 'breaking' the 'engagement,' we'll have told so many lies I won't remember which is which!"

"Dave may not be sure he wants to break it off." Netta dropped her bombshell as calmly as if she were discussing the weather.

"What?" Merrie splashed chocolate across the coffee table and had to mop it up with her napkin.

"I think he's smitten with you," Netta continued. "Mind you, I'm not suggesting he's trying to trick you into anything. But perhaps the thought has crossed his mind that in time the two of you might seriously want to consider getting married."

Merrie shook her head. "I can't imagine it. Netta, if you'd seen his house—I could never live there. It would be like moving into the Taj Mahal!"

"If that's your only objection, things might not be as hopeless as they seem." Without giving her a chance to protest, Netta stood up. "I'll be expecting the five of you for brunch tomorrow—I don't suppose that hotel's kitchen is geared up yet. Now get some rest."

"I'll try." But Merrie lay awake late that night, trying to sort out her tangled thoughts.

She would simply have to insist that Dave tell his mother the truth, immediately. There was no other possible course, Merrie decided at last, and finally drifted into sleep.

She'd reckoned without Dave, who seemed determined to avoid the subject.

On Sunday, after a memorable brunch of Netta's homestyle muffins, French toast, and omelets, he excused himself, pleading a prior engagement. Merrie was left to take her three charges to the airport and bid a tearful farewell to Steffie, promising solemnly to take good care of Puddles until the little girl returned.

Her only glimmer of pleasure came from Drum's parting words. "She really does seem attached to you. I wasn't sure, when Lizabeth suggested she attend school in Nashville, but it might not be a bad idea."

"She could learn a lot about class from Sarah Anders," Lizabeth added, apparently oblivious to the implication that the child couldn't learn class from Merrie.

But Merrie knew her sister too well to take offense. Besides, even as she watched the little family disappear through the boarding gate, she was already planning what she would say to Dave when she telephoned him that night.

But when she called, his familiar voice answered on

the second ring, "Hello. Sorry I'm not home to take your call . . ."

As soon as the beep sounded, Merrie snapped, "Call me," and hung up. She was sure he would figure out who it was.

He didn't call.

Instead, arriving at the clinic bleary-eyed the next morning after a restless night, she was greeted by the sight of a dozen red roses on her desk.

"They came a few minutes ago," Alida Reese called from the reception room. "No card."

"Secret admirer?" Bill Brown leaned in the doorway. Her partner was tall and slender, with a wispy mustache and a direct gaze that invariably put children and pets at ease.

"It would take me all day to explain," Merrie muttered, glaring at the flowers as if they were skunkweed.

"By the way, how's your head?" Sue must have told him about the racquetball match.

"It only throbbed for a few hours." Merrie sighed. "I think I'd better get to work and forget all about this weekend. It was a disaster."

She managed to bury herself in work for most of the day, but the roses nagged at her. Every time she stepped into her office, Merrie had the uncomfortable sensation that Dave was watching.

He'd better call tonight, that's all I can say.

But he didn't. And when she telephoned his office on Tuesday, his secretary said he was out of town.

And that was how the week went. Flowers arrived daily; puppy biscuits turned up on her front porch, along with three beribboned bags of catnip; once a prepaid pizza was delivered to her door just as she arrived home, and Merrie waited half an hour before attacking it, expecting that surely Dave would arrive to share the feast.

No such luck.

At home, his machine continued to answer the phone. His secretary assured Merrie that he was out of town indefinitely. The florist, when contacted, informed her that the purchaser of the flowers had insisted that no information be given out, so she couldn't even learn whether he'd placed a standing order or was dropping by daily to pick out the cheerful sprays of daisies, roses, baby's breath, and chrysanthemums.

On Friday, an announcement of the engagement appeared in the newspaper, accompanied by an old photograph of Merrie that must have come from the newspaper files. She'd sent it in four years ago, when she and Bill announced that they were taking over the Brown Animal Center.

A written message, obviously hand-delivered since it bore no postmark, was waiting at Merrie's house that evening. It said: "Don't worry about the guest list. We called Netta today and it's all taken care of." There was no signature.

Merrie stormed next door, where a perplexed Netta said she'd given a list of names and addresses to Dave's secretary, who'd assured her Merrie was aware of the arrangements.

"This has to stop." Merrie glared at one of Netta's African violets, as if all flowers had gone over to the enemy. "Netta, it isn't even that I intend to cancel the party; it's too late for that. We might as well keep up this 'engagement' until Steffie's settled in with me and Lizabeth's too busy to change her mind. But I don't like the feeling I'm being railroaded."

"I suspect that, if you really want to, you'll find a way to flush him out." Netta refused to say any more.

On Saturday morning, Merrie woke up knowing what she had to do. Maybe it had come to her in a dream, or maybe her thoughts had simply sorted themselves out overnight, but she dialed the phone and told Dave's answering machine, "If you aren't over here by five o'clock this afternoon, I'm calling your mother and telling her everything. And I don't care if you *are* out of town. You'd better get on the next plane."

There were, after all, devices for picking up machine messages by remote control, and she had no doubt that a man as efficient as Dave must possess one.

Fortunately for Merrie's nerves, she didn't have to wait until five o'clock. In fact, she was still lingering over her coffee and toast when the doorbell rang.

"I don't believe it." She addressed the comment to Puddles, who was romping on the floor to the lazy amusement of Homebody.

But in spite of the fact that she'd been trying to hunt Dave down all week, Merrie wasn't prepared for the sheer physical impact of confronting him when she opened the door.

A red plaid hunter's jacket over corduroy jeans emphasized the masculine huskiness of his body, and a light breeze conspired to ruffle his hair with engaging boyishness. "Got your message." Dave's mouth twitched, and she gathered he was struggling to hide a smile. "Something bothering you?"

"You're outrageous, infuriating, arrogant, and irresponsible." Merrie glared at him.

"I object to 'irresponsible.'" He moved past her without waiting for an invitation. "I made sure we had your friends and relations on the guest list, didn't I?"

"Yes, but—" Merrie chased after him into the kitchen, where Dave was hoisting the delighted puppy overhead. "Now, look—"

"You're doing a terrific job with him. What's your secret?" Dave cuddled the little animal against his jacket. "Lots of TLC and good home cooking?"

"Put the dog down." With an effort, Merrie kept her tone level. "We are going to have a serious discussion, and you are not going to keep interrupting me or changing the subject."

"Did you like the flowers?" Despite his cheeky air, Dave set the puppy on the floor and let Merrie point him into the living room. Unfortunately, Puddles danced about his ankles, spoiling the solemnity of the moment, until Merrie shut the protesting puppy into the utility room.

"I thought we had an agreement." Merrie stalked into the living room, where Dave had draped himself over the sofa. Towering over him gave her a certain psychological advantage, and she needed it. "This engagement was a hoax to fool my sister."

"Have I said otherwise?"

She ignored the remark. "Furthermore, I made it quite plain I wasn't interested in getting involved in a relationship. You agreed to let me handle things my way."

"I did?" In spite of his serious expression, he was obviously taking everything she said with a very large chunk of salt.

"Dave, I'm not kidding!"

"First of all, Merrie, I think you should sit down." He accompanied his words with an unexpected tug at her hand that threw her off balance. Stumbling, she was easy prey for a second tug, which landed her at his side. "Second, the chemistry between us is powerful enough to make Madame Curie take note."

"She was a physicist," Merrie interjected.

"Precisely." Sliding one arm around her shoulders,

Dave pressed his verbal attack. "We're fooling with elemental stuff here. Resistance is useless, Merrie. You, of all people, should know that nature has to take its course."

"You're so full of hot air I'm surprised you don't float." Several more sharp retorts started up to her lips but never made their way out, because Dave's mouth was blocking their exit.

As his kiss breathed fire into her veins and his hands worked a slow, irresistible magic on her shoulders and back, the rebellious thought surfaced that maybe Dave was right.

Why had she tried to keep him at a distance? Merrie wondered as his breath warmed her cheek and his body pressed close to hers, mastering without dominating, tantalizing without pressuring. He felt so right in her arms, in her house, and her heart.

He was right about the chemistry, too, was the last rational thought she had all evening.

Her body took over, freed at last from the chains of Merrie's intellect. It knew that skin belonged against skin, that his muscles would tempt her fingers unbearably, that his hands would free them both to lie unabashedly side by side, with no clothing to interrupt the flow of electricity that sizzled between them.

This was neither chemistry nor physics but alchemy, the magical transmutation of base metals into gold. The everyday Merrie was lifted into an ethereal world of shimmering rainbows, through which Dave cut like a sword of light. She burned beneath his touch, aching to enter realms that had never beckoned to her before. Only Dave could take her there . . . only Dave . . .

They joined as rivulets of fire, sparking against a midnight sky, heating the horizon into sunrise brilliance. All the elements of the alchemist filled her: sulfur and silver, lead and mercury, forging a new, precious metal that was the union of Merrie and Dave.

Together they raced across undiscovered worlds and charted the unexplored hollows of the universe. Time stretched and folded upon itself, and sensation had no beginning, no end, nor any limit.

When the fire muted into embers, Merrie lay quietly in Dave's arms, her eyes closed against the intrusion of the ordinary. She knew instinctively that among the last ashes of desire she would find drops of pure gold, the consummation of the alchemy.

"As I was saying," Dave murmured against her ear, "it's best to let nature take its course."

Merrie's lips on his were the only answer either of them required.

CHAPTER
Ten

"IS HE GOING TO DIE, doctor?" The boy peered anxiously up at Merrie, his small face barely higher than the examining table.

"No. But it's a good thing you brought him in." Merrie finished cleaning the cat's wound and bandaged it carefully. Despite its lop-eared, tough-guy appearance, the raggedy cat looked meek now, under a mild anesthetic. She was glad she had a job this rewarding and this absorbing, or it would have been difficult to concentrate on anything except thoughts of Dave this past week, since they'd become lovers.

"He's not really mine." The little boy was almost as scruffy as the cat, his T-shirt torn and his hair sticking up near the crown. "He sort of lives near us. But he's my friend."

A cherished friend, Merrie gathered, since the boy had brought the cat all the way across Nashville on a bus to be treated. He was one of the foster children she'd met at the Christmas party, and although she didn't remember him, he'd certainly remembered her. Fortunately for the cat.

"Now, Peter, your cat's going to need to stay indoors until this heals. And the wound needs to be cleaned and redressed. I'll give you the supplies, but do you think you can follow instructions?" The boy was small for his age—he said he was ten—but obviously bright.

"My foster mom said he could sleep in the garage." Peter dug his hands into his pockets. "But I don't have much to pay you with. Do I owe you a lot?"

Merrie shook her head sympathetically. "I'll tell you what. You keep a lookout for a child or animal who needs your help, and that's how you'll repay me. Okay?"

As the boy nodded, she could see him tucking away this debt of honor, never to be forgotten. Working Saturdays wasn't Merrie's favorite thing to do, and she'd been on the run all day, but moments like this made it more than worthwhile.

Most of her free time this past week had been absorbed by planning the party—one of the highlights of the social season, a newspaper article had called it—but the highlights of *her* social season were the precious, rare evenings when they could relax together, making love, sipping hot chocolate in front of Merrie's fireplace, sharing private jokes.

Yet Merrie had also caught a troubling glimpse of another Dave. She had dropped by his office to join him for lunch on Thursday, and she'd seen him in action with an associate, making rapid-fire decisions that involved huge sums of money, his whole being focused on the subject at hand, his muscles tightening so that even the planes of his face became unfamiliar. There'd been a hint of that arrogance she'd sensed at their first meeting, when he ordered Alida to release his dog after closing time. But of course, he wasn't really like that. Everyone acted different at work than at home.

Merrie snapped out of her reverie as the cat whimpered and stared dazedly around. "Are you sure you can carry him back on the bus? I'll be done here in about half an hour."

"No, it's okay." The boy's chin came up proudly. He

was someone special, torn T-shirt and all. "I like animals. Maybe someday I'll be a vet like you. I guess you have to go to school for a long time, huh?"

"A lot like a people doctor." Merrie began washing up. "You know, a long time ago, the same doctors took care of people and animals both."

"They did?" Peter stroked the cat to reassure it.

Merrie enjoyed the opportunity to teach a little about her profession, and Peter was obviously an eager audience. "In fact, veterinarians have discovered a lot of things that are important to people. Like how some diseases are transmitted. And the artificial hip was first developed for dogs by a veterinarian."

"That's what I'm going to be." Peter lifted down his cat. "A veterinarian."

Merrie would have liked to talk with him some more, but Jenny, the teenager who worked at the clinic part-time, appeared in the doorway. "There's a lady here with a Great Dane. She thinks it's got a broken leg."

Merrie groaned inwardly. Setting a leg in a large animal like that was no simple matter. She'd be here later than she'd expected.

But as she gave Peter the supplies he needed for the cat, she realized that she didn't mind.

Sure, it was exciting to plan a glamorous party and to be the center of attention. And even more, she loved being with Dave. But an essential part of Merrie belonged here, where she was needed.

Smiling to herself, she went out to see about the Great Dane.

Who were all these people?

Merrie stood to one side of Dave's vast living room, half hidden by a streamer of red and white Valentine's Day balloons that sagged from its upper mooring. Sunday afternoon sunlight flooded through the great front windows.

The large rooms were crowded with gaily dressed Nashvilleans, their chatter overwhelming the delicate love songs played by a string trio tucked into one corner. As Dave had planned, people stayed in motion between the three bars and two food tables, never settling in one place long enough to block what he'd termed the "flow of traffic." Uniformed maids passed among the knots of people, offering trays of champagne and hors d'oeuvres.

The only people Merrie had taken into her confidence about the fake engagement besides Netta were Bill and Sue Brown. She peered into the throng, trying to spot them, but failed to locate their reassuringly familiar faces.

"*Ma chèrie*, everything is *très charmant, n'est-ce pas?*" Gigi appeared at Merrie's elbow, her French phrases pronounced with a disconcerting Southern accent. She'd only arrived late last night, and Merrie hadn't quite gotten reaccustomed to her mother's ways yet.

"I'm glad you're here." As she said the words, Merrie realized they were true. "Mom, I wish we saw each other more often. We haven't even had a chance to talk."

"Talk? What is talk?" Gigi waved her hand airily. "When my daughter makes a brilliant marriage, who needs to talk? *Chèrie*, even your sister is impressed! Such a handsome man, and such a fine home! You have made quite a catch!"

Merrie's indulgent smile froze on her face as she caught sight of a woman nearby, turning away in obvious distaste. The woman was one of Sarah Anders's closest friends. Instantly, Merrie realized how her mother's words must have sounded—as if Merrie were a gold digger who had snared herself a rich prize.

She wanted to disappear. But Lizabeth and Drum were at hand, requiring her attention. Merrie did her best to look cheerful.

"Everybody, but *everybody* is here!" Lizabeth at least had the sense to keep her voice down. "Even the mayor! Drum's made some terrific contacts."

"Maybe I'd better go check on Steffie," Merrie said. The little girl was being tended by a baby-sitter upstairs. "I've hardly had a chance to see her." Lizabeth, Drum, and Gigi had checked into their hotel late last night, and Steffie had been asleep by the time Merrie joined them for a nightcap. This morning, the child—wearing a frilly pink dress that had probably cost a small fortune—had been whisked upstairs after only a few minutes.

"No need for that. She's well taken care of." Drum obviously considered a child to be a poor reason to leave a party.

"He's absolutely right." Lizabeth leaned closer to examine Merrie's pearl-and-diamond earrings. No doubt she assumed they were a gift from Dave, but actually Merrie had bought them for herself on her twenty-ninth birthday. "How stunning. You've outdone yourself, sweetie!" Her gaze took in Merrie's understated white silk dress and stylishly trimmed hair. "Real class. And your hair! Brushed up that way, it makes you look like Princess Diana."

"Dave arranged for a hairdresser to come to my house this morning." Merrie shifted uncomfortably. "Really, I never expected the party to be so elaborate. It seems sort of—" She was about to say *excessive*, but realized that would sound like criticism of Dave and Sarah.

"*Ma chérie*, you always were too modest," Gigi scolded.

"You can't fool us," Lizabeth added. "You looked radiant in the receiving line when we came in. Now admit it—you're enjoying this!"

"Up to a point." That was certainly true. Selecting her dress, admiring the sumptuous flower arrangements, watching the first guests arrive—those things had indeed appealed to Merrie's sense of wonder. An hour ago, standing between Dave and Sarah Anders in the front hall, she'd felt a bit like Cinderella, light-headed from the delicate scents of spring blossoms and expensive perfume.

Why had the magic vanished? Maybe it had been crushed beneath the weight of her conscience, she acknowledged silently. Oh, heavens, how did she ever let things get so out of hand?

She needed Dave, needed his strength and warmth right now to assuage the pangs of guilt. Up till now, he'd managed somehow to make her feel as if this whole charade was perfectly all right.

Sometimes Merrie had the impression that Dave was, indeed, taking this engagement as something more than a hoax. But despite the warnings crying out from the back of her mind, she hadn't been ready to talk about the future. Not yet. Not while everything between them was so new and gossamer and enchanted.

There he was, heading toward her, his broad shoulders fitting perfectly into the classic black tuxedo, his gray eyes fixing on each person he passed just long enough to give the impression each had been well and thoroughly noticed.

Merrie's heart swelled with joy as Dave reached her side. "Everyone surviving?" he teased as his arm encircled her waist. His thumb caressed her hip lightly, raising chills across her flesh at the memory of the night before last. Friday night. They'd made love in this house, in his den . . .

"Honey." Sarah Anders joined them, including Merrie's family in her polite nod, but singling out her son at the same time. "Kip's ready to propose a toast."

Can't we skip this part? Merrie tried to signal Dave by squeezing his hand, but he was already leading her toward the main refreshment table, where Kip waited with a glass at the ready. Sarah Anders stayed behind, her expression unreadable, as Gigi chattered about some teacher they'd known in high school.

"Dave." It was hard to whisper in his ear while they were in motion, but Merrie tried. "Look, Lizabeth and Drum are convinced, and that was the point, right? Can't we manage to blow a fuse and send everyone home?"

"We've got to play this out to the end." Dave averted his eyes, smiling at an acquaintance as they passed. "You want my mother to get her money's worth, don't you?"

Merrie shivered. This party must have cost thousands of dollars. She promised herself silently to reimburse Sarah Anders once Steffie was settled and the truth could be told. The expenditure would hurt, but it would assuage her conscience.

They reached Kip, and he tapped a spoon against his glass for silence. A wave of "*shshshshsh*"-ing spread through the crowd, and the string trio fell silent.

"I'd like to propose a toast." The room rang with the scrape and ping of fine crystal being raised. "To the best friend a man could ever hope for, Dave Anders, and his beautiful bride-to-be, Merrie McGregor."

"Dave and Merrie!" the names were almost indistinguishable in the many-throated mumble. Her cheeks stinging, Merrie stared in front of her and finally spotted Netta. Her grandmother was shaking her head sympathetically. Beside her, Bill Brown lifted his champagne glass and winked at Merrie, which made her feel a shade better.

Then Dave stepped to Kip's side. "And I'd like us all to drink to a monkey named Britches, without whom Merrie and I would never have gotten acquainted." There were speculative grins as the crowd again joined the toast.

Merrie, too, took a sip, relieved that the informal ceremony was over.

Except that Dave was holding up his hand for silence. "One more thing, folks. I'd like to present my future wife with a small token of my esteem." As Merrie watched in disbelief, Kip produced a jewelry box and Dave opened it to reveal a ring that sparkled and caught the light. An appreciative buzz rose from the crowd.

I can't accept this. The words caught in her throat. Of course, the ring could be returned later, couldn't it? But why had Dave gone to such lengths?

An unexpected surge of anger boiled through Merrie, heating her cheeks and rendering her momentarily speechless. He'd tricked her. Did he really think she could be manipulated into marrying him? Spending their lives together was an issue that needed to be carefully considered, not something he could thrust on her highhandedly.

She might have snapped at him and ruined everything, except that in the silence as the guests awaited her response, Merrie heard a dog bark upstairs. Buster. Playing with Steffie.

The little girl's happiness lay in Merrie's hands. Furious as she was with Dave's arrogance, there was no point in blowing off steam right now. After all, he couldn't *force* her to marry him.

"How lovely." She hoped the others would attribute her choked voice to tender emotion. "I—I wasn't expecting this."

"This is a very special ring." Sarah Anders materialized at Merrie's side. "The diamonds come from an heirloom necklace that belonged to my grandmother. Dave had the setting specially designed."

How *could* he have done this? Merrie didn't trust herself to say anything, so she pretended to be absorbed in examining the ring as Dave slipped it on her finger. A perfect fit; he must have found some sneaky way to measure her finger, or else he'd borrowed one of the costume jewelry rings she sometimes wore. She wouldn't put anything past him, at this point.

Fortunately, Lizabeth and Drum provided a welcome distraction as they made their way toward her through the crowd.

Sarah Anders was speaking again. "We have one more happy announcement to make today. For those of you who haven't met them, this is Merrie's sister Lizabeth and her fiancé, Drummond Haymes III."

Lizabeth reached them and swung around to face the guests. Tall and radiant in rose silk, she looked positively regal. "I hope my sister doesn't mind sharing just a tiny bit of her spotlight—Mrs. Anders didn't think you'd mind, Merrie. You see, Drum and I have decided to get married in two weeks, at the new Haymes Hotel-Nashville, and we'd like everyone here to be our guests. One P.M. in the ballroom. I know it's short notice, but our mother's here from France, and we didn't want her to have to make two trips."

A round of applause greeted the news. Merrie gave

her sister a hug, her spirits finally lifting as she realized what this might mean.

Once Lizabeth and Drum were married, they'd be going on their honeymoon. And then they'd be absorbed in each other. Which meant they'd probably want to get Steffie settled as soon as possible. And after today, there was little doubt the child would be entrusted to Merrie.

At least some good would come of all this deception.

Netta and Gigi surged forward for hugs and kisses all around, and the guests began to refill their plates and glasses. Finally, Merrie decamped for the powder room, and Lizabeth caught up with her in the hall.

"You didn't mind, did you?" Lizabeth's radiant smile dimmed a fraction. "About us barging in with our announcement?"

"Not at all." And Merrie meant it unreservedly. "But what about Drum's family? Can they get here on such short notice?"

"That was part of what made us decide." Lizabeth glanced about to be sure they weren't overheard. "You see, he's sure they wouldn't want to attend—looks too much like a stamp of approval. They'd just send one of his sisters or an aunt, as a token to show the family wasn't objecting to the marriage, either. So he wants to one-up them by making it so they couldn't attend even if they wanted to. Drum's got a lot of pride, and I think he wants to spare my feelings, too. Isn't that sweet?"

"He's a good man." Merrie only wished she felt more certain he'd be a good father for Steffie.

"And of course you'll be my maid of honor. Won't you? Dave's already agreed to be best man! We thought we'd keep it in the family."

"Of course I will." There was a lot to think about—a bridesmaid's dress, perhaps a shower—but Merrie realized she was almost getting used to having her life in an uproar. "Had you thought about the arrangements for Steffie?"

"Oh, she'll be the flower girl." Then Merrie's meaning penetrated. "You mean afterward? If you don't mind, maybe she can stay with you. We're going to Fiji for the honeymoon! And next fall, well, I think you're right. She *would* be better off boarding with you, if you haven't changed your mind."

Not likely! "I'd be thrilled to have her."

The rest of the party passed in a blur. Merrie's anger at Dave continued to burn despite her happiness over Steffie, and it took all her energy to appear cheerful as guests paused to congratulate her and exclaim over the ring. It seemed like hours before everyone left, and Merrie, Dave, and Sarah were finally alone, supervising the caterers' assistants and the maids as they cleaned up.

"My dear." Sarah laid her hand on Merrie's arm. "I must confess that at first I was taken aback when I learned of this engagement so suddenly. But now that I've come to know you, I must say that I'm delighted."

The unexpected compliment sent a wave of guilt washing over Merrie. *I can't keep on lying to her,* she thought. "Mrs. Anders, that's very, very kind of you. But there's something I think we should talk about."

Dave, standing half a dozen feet away, was facing the kitchen, telling the caterers where to stow the leftovers. But he spun around at Merrie's words. "I think you two can wait for your little heart-to-heart, don't you?"

"No, I don't," Merrie said.

Sarah Anders studied them both, clearly picking up the strain in their voices. "I think perhaps you two should be the ones to talk privately. My dear Merrie, we'll have plenty of time to get better acquainted. I'll take care of things here; Dave, why don't you take Merrie home?"

And so she found herself bundled off in the Mercedes, feeling even frostier than the February landscape. Merrie kept silent as they drove, not trusting herself to let loose in such an enclosed space.

Her fury had mounted to fever pitch by the time they arrived in her living room, but it was Dave who spoke first.

"You ought to thank me for saving you from your own heedlessness. Do you know what might have happened if you'd spilled the beans to my mother?"

"That's exactly why—"

"With Lizabeth and Drum's wedding only two weeks off, you want to spoil everything now?" he confronted her, the few feet between them vibrating with tension. "What happened to your concern for Steffie?"

"Lizabeth's already agreed to leave her with me!" Merrie flared. "All right. Maybe right now isn't a good time to tell your mother. But I feel rotten, deceiving her this way! And that stunt with the ring was unforgivable. You actually had your great-grandmother's diamonds reset?"

"They look nice, don't you think?" Dave reached out, tilting her hand so the ring glinted. "Merrie, don't you see what it signifies? Unlike Drum's family, mine has accepted my bride completely."

"Aren't you forgetting something?" She snatched her hand away. "This whole thing is a fake! We aren't really getting married . . ."

"Why not?" Dave planted himself squarely in front of her. "We're happy together, aren't we? At least, that's the impression you gave me . . ." One finger traced the curve of her cheek until Merrie jumped back.

"You have one hell of a big ego!" She wasn't about

to let herself get sidetracked, not even by the instinctive heat that prickled her skin at his touch. "That was arrogant, getting the ring without asking me first!"

"I made an executive decision." He shrugged. "Would it help if I apologize? Then we can forget this pointless argument and get on with our wedding plans."

"There isn't going to be any wedding." Merrie couldn't disguise her anguish. "Dave, we're wrong for each other. That party today—I can't live like that. That's not my world."

"Give it a chance." He brushed aside her objections impatiently. "You know what I think is really bothering you? It's your pride. You're afraid people will think you're a social climber. Well, anyone who knows you would find that laughable."

Maybe that *was* a small part of what concerned her, but certainly not all of it. "Dave, I know I'm not explaining this very well, but look at my house! Sure, you enjoy visiting here, but would you really want to live this way?"

Dave shook his head impatiently. "We don't have to live here. My house is big enough for us and Steffie and a whole menagerie."

"It's too big! And all that formal furniture—"

"Are we really arguing about my decor? I don't believe this." Dave cut her off, his voice rough with annoyance. "Merrie, you don't give yourself enough credit. You can manage your career and be the perfect hostess at the same time; you were stunning today. My friends kept congratulating me on finding such a beauty."

"I don't want—"

"Let me finish." Infuriatingly, he didn't seem to notice that he wasn't letting *her* finish a sentence. "We belong together, and you know it. If you can honestly say that you could never love me, then I'll walk right out of here forever."

"Dave, I don't know—"

"Well, I do. And I don't believe in wasting time."

"Dammit, I'm not one of your employees, and I'm not a subsidiary to be bought and sold, either!" Merrie flashed out. "You made an executive decision? How dare you! Who elected you chairman of the board around here?"

For the first time since they'd arrived, Dave didn't have an immediate answer. He opened his mouth, and then closed it again. Finally, he said in a milder tone, "I love you, Merrie."

"Do you?" She had to fight back the tears. "Or do you just love the woman you think I could be? The beautiful hostess, or whatever it is you want."

"Maybe I got a little carried away a few minutes ago." He stepped toward her, but Merrie moved quickly away. "I guess I *was* operating like the president of a company instead of like a lover. But I want you to think it over. We can talk more when we've calmed down."

"All right." Suddenly, Merrie needed urgently to be alone. "Later, Dave."

She ducked as he leaned toward her, and he brushed a kiss across her temple. "Congratulations about Steffie."

"Thanks." Merrie didn't trust herself to look up until she heard his footsteps cross the room and the front door close quietly behind him. Feeling like a wild animal torn between a comfortable captivity and a lonely freedom, she stalked upstairs to take off her dress.

The realization forced itself upon her as she pulled off the gown: She loved Dave. Even now, through the tatters of her anger, she missed him.

It was so tempting.

Merrie brushed out her hair, trying to imagine herself living in that grand house. What was so wrong with compromise, after all?

The problem was, she wasn't sure they were really talking about compromise. In her heart, it felt more like surrender.

Dave was perfect for her in so many ways. But she'd only known him for—what—less than two months. Not time enough to understand that other, domineering side of him.

How ironic that she'd fled New York and flouted her mother and sister only to find herself swept back into their world. Could she really be happy there, even with Dave at her side?

Merrie mulled over that question all evening, without being able to dispel the unease that lingered in her soul.

CHAPTER
Eleven

"I DON'T KNOW—veils are so, well, old-fashioned."
Lizabeth examined herself in the dress-shop mirror. The
white lacy gown with its unusual square-cut sleeves and
low waistline fitted her perfectly, which was probably
the first time that had happened in the history of the
store. And a good thing, Merrie reflected, since there
was only a week left until the wedding, not much time
for alterations.

"I don't like the veil, Mommy." Steffie, wiggling
uncomfortably in her pink flower girl's dress, frowned
into the mirror.

"That does it." Flashing a mischievous smile at the
saleslady, Lizabeth ripped off the veil and reached for a
perky white hat with silk roses curling across the brim.
"Now, how do you like that?"

As the little girl chirped her approval, Merrie found
herself relaxing for the first time since her argument
with Dave. She'd tried to keep busy this week, and it
hadn't been difficult—after work, she'd helped Lizabeth mail the hastily printed invitations, arrange for
flowers, and pick out the menu that would give the
hotel's staff a needed trial run. The wedding had been
scheduled for one day before the official opening, and
Drum was obviously killing two birds with one stone.

But no matter how many activities Merrie crammed
into a day, the nights belonged to thoughts of Dave—to

the memory of his touch, of their lovemaking, of his most unromantic proposal. The discomfort she felt at the prospect of living in his house, according to his lifestyle, had, if anything, intensified. But so had her visceral need to feel his arms around her and to hear his voice.

"I like your dress, Aunt Merrie." Steffie's words provided a welcome interruption to Merrie's thoughts.

"Do you? So do I." Smoothing down the deep rose silk of the gown, Merrie moved forward to stand beside her sister in the triptych of mirrors. They were almost the same height—Lizabeth perhaps an inch taller—and built similarly, with the slim neck and slender frame of a model. And their coloring was gently complementary, Lizabeth's ash-blond mane and Merrie's short strawberry-blond curls reminding Merrie of pastel flowers blooming side-by-side in a garden.

But there was a radiance about Lizabeth that Merrie could only envy from a far emotional distance. Even her joy at the prospect of making a home for Steffie couldn't duplicate the glow that love had brought to Lizabeth.

"Oh, Merrie!" Lizabeth swung around and clasped her arm. "Can you believe this is really happening? And next it will be your turn! I plan to be your matron of honor, you know."

"Of course." Merrie ducked her head, hoping her sister would mistake her flushed cheeks for a sign of excitement.

"We'll take the dresses! And the hat, too," Lizabeth told the saleswoman. "And my sister's getting married next, so I imagine we'll be back."

"We have new stock coming in almost daily," the woman responded, clearly delighted by the order. "These are some of our newest spring fashions, and of course the summer styles will be here soon."

Lizabeth glanced around the shop. "Oh, and I'll take those white lace stockings, too. Do you have pink ones in children's sizes? Terrific. I think it's so clever of you to carry flower girl dresses; we must have looked in a dozen children's stores . . ."

With all the chatter and the wrapping, it was a good half hour before they left the store, and Steffie loudly proclaimed that she was starving.

"Drum's expecting us for lunch." Lizabeth tossed the packages into the back of the station wagon. "Merrie, won't you join us?"

"Thanks, but Saturday's my housecleaning day and I'd better not put it off or I might disappear in a mountain of cat hair." Merrie steered toward the hotel to drop off her passengers. "And I want to hang some new curtains in Steffie's room, so it'll be all ready when she moves in." Steffie would be leaving the hotel and coming to Merrie's house right after the wedding.

Lizabeth didn't seem to mind Merrie's not staying for lunch; but then, she was operating in a perpetual state of bliss these days, Merrie mused as she waved good-bye to her sister and Steffie.

Bliss was definitely not the word for how Merrie felt an hour later, a scarf wrapped around her head and the vacuum cleaner roaring in her ears. She almost wished she'd declined Bill's generous offer to fill in at the clinic, even though it was her turn. Anything would be better than this; and to make matters worse, this was the first springlike day in months, its sunshine beckoning Merrie to take a stroll. But there was no point in postponing the inevitable. Dirt had never been known to disappear by itself.

A burst of yipping from Puddles halted Merrie, and

she switched off the vacuum. Immediately, she heard the muted chimes of the doorbell.

Oh, no. One hand reaching up to snatch away the grimy bandanna, Merrie peered out a side window to see who was at the door.

Dave.

Her heart did a series of leaps. Quickly, Merrie surveyed the living room, noting with approval its freshly polished furniture and newly cleaned upholstery. The only problem was that all the dirt had migrated onto the mistress of the house.

The chimes rang again.

Well, she couldn't ignore him. And besides, Merrie felt an urgency that shattered her best-laid arguments; she simply couldn't wait another instant to see Dave.

She flung open the door, acutely aware of what a disheveled sight she must be. "Hi."

His expression mutated from surprise to amusement. "Gee, I hope you didn't go to all this trouble on my account."

Merrie tried to think of a clever response, but she couldn't. She was too busy sorting out her first reaction, which felt something like a forest fire raging inside a dusty broom closet. "I've missed you."

"Do you think I might come in?" He was grinning, and Merrie stepped hastily aside, aware that she'd been gaping at him like an adolescent. She tried to focus on something prosaic—the thick wool of his Scandinavian knit sweater, the wicker basket over one arm, the guitar slung over one shoulder. A wicker basket and a guitar?

"What's that stuff for?" Merrie reached up to flick a bit of lint off her forehead and was dismayed to find dirt on her hand when she lifted it away.

"A picnic lunch."

"A picnic? In February?"

"I'll tell you what." Dave set the basket on a side table and steered Merrie toward the stairs. "You go clean up and we'll discuss this later."

"Well—I *am* hungry." And with that concession, she headed for the shower.

By the time Merrie came down again in a pair of jeans and a sweater, Dave had filled her Thermos with hot chocolate. In the backyard, she noticed, through the kitchen window, he'd spread out a colorful old blanket from Merrie's linen closet

"There's a bit of a chill in the air," he warned as he led the way outside. "But I love picnics."

The sunlight felt warm on Merrie's shoulders, although the light breeze did indeed still hint at winter. "So do I."

"How about a truce?" Dave knelt on the blanket and began removing food from the basket. "For the next few hours, we forget about everything except the here and now."

"The ravenous will agree to anything." Merrie reached for a piece of fried chicken. "Don't tell me you cooked this yourself?"

"A special order from the Loveless Motel." Dave winked as he mentioned the name of the establishment just outside Nashville that was famous for its Southern cooking. "Actually, I'd say it was a lover's delight, wouldn't you?"

"It's one of my favorite places." Merrie began smearing butter and honey on a biscuit. "This stuff beats gourmet cooking hands down."

Dave poured the hot chocolate into mugs and handed Merrie a napkin. "Lunch will be followed by a concert."

"You really play the guitar?" She eyed the instrument dubiously. "A Yamaha? Do you strum it or ride it?"

"Hey. I'm a native of Nashville. Of course I play the

guitar." Dave waved a drumstick. "I beat out tunes with my fried chicken, down-home style."

"You goofball." Merrie found herself chuckling help-lessly. This was the side of Dave she adored. And found irresistible. And wasn't sure she could live without. If only he didn't have the other side to him. But then, she'd promised not to think about that today.

"You big-city girls don't look down on us country musicians, do you?" Dave finished his meal and wiped his hands on a towel.

"My dad was a country musician." Merrie hesitated. She didn't talk about her father often; she'd hardly known him. "He died when I was seven. Sometimes I wonder what my life would have been like if he'd lived."

"You weren't close to your stepfather?" Dave began tuning the guitar.

"Which one?" Merrie watched, intrigued, as he bent to listen to the tones. "To answer your question, no. Mom remarried a few years later and left us with Grandma Netta, and when she got divorced, she stayed on in New York."

"So you want to make sure Steffie isn't cheated out of a family life the way you were." His face was averted as he tuned an errant string.

"Something like that." Merrie hugged her knees, resting her cheek atop them. "What do you think of Drum?"

"As a father, you mean? Hard to tell." Dave strummed the guitar idly. "I like the way he sticks up for Lizabeth, planning the wedding so his family can't play its snobbish games on her."

"But he never talks about his own children," Merrie pointed out.

"Not to you. But how well do you know him?" Dave

began picking out a melody that Merrie couldn't place. "He seems like a good man. Beyond that, we'll have to wait and see."

We. Was he making assumptions? Somehow Merrie didn't feel like debating the point. In fact, it was reassuring that Dave seemed to be counting himself in when it came to Steffie's future.

The melody he was playing did sound vaguely familiar. Merrie tried to concentrate. It had a whimsical, almost childish quality...

"Oh!" Merrie stared at him accusingly. "That's 'I Saw Mommy Kissing Santa,' isn't it?"

"Is it?" He widened his eyes in pretended innocence. "Gee, I wasn't sure what it was. Tunes just sort of drift through my mind, you know."

"You conniver!" Merrie scooped up the last biscuit and nibbled at it, curbing the impulse to heave it at him. "How about 'Rhapsody in Blue'?"

"That's a piano piece."

"Just testing." She considered for a moment. "Well, how about 'Malagueña'?"

"Let's try some genuine American folk songs. There must be one that's appropriate to the occasion." Dave frowned as if in deep thought, then swung into a lilting waltz rhythm. Merrie half closed her eyes, prepared to listen to a romantic ballad in Dave's husky baritone, but her eyelids popped open again as he launched into a ditty entitled "My Sweetheart's a Mule."

"Wait a minute!"

Dave ignored her as he repeated a verse about sitting in back of the mule and spitting tobacco all over his sweetheart's behind.

"Is that supposed to be funny?" It was, actually, but Merrie was doing her best not to laugh.

"Gee, the folks down home like it." Without pausing, he segued into a song about hog drovers, which featured an exaggerated Tennessee accent and some most unmusical oinks between stanzas.

"You're making these up!" Merrie poked him in the ribs, unable to stop herself from giggling as he produced a fair imitation of a disgruntled piglet.

"Why, I thought you'd love some songs about animals. It's in your honor, Doc." Dave twisted away to avoid her next poke, and stopped playing. "Actually, those are real folk songs. They've withstood the test of time."

"You actually perform those in public?"

"With a lampshade on my head. I'm the hit of my friends' parties." Setting the guitar aside, Dave twined an arm around Merrie's waist. "How about some spooning, sweetheart?"

"Grandma Netta lives right next door!"

"She's not my type." Without waiting for her indignant response, Dave pulled Merrie off-balance and dashed a kiss across her lips as she flopped against him.

"Hey!" She tried to regain her balance, but he was running his hands mischievously across her curves under the pretense of trying to help her up.

"Are you all right?" One hand slid beneath her sweater, burning a fiery trail up her back. "Can I help you?" The other hand stroked across her inner thigh, the heat of his body sizzling through Merrie's jeans.

"Dave, if you don't—"

"Oh, well, if you insist." With a well-placed push, he landed Merrie flat on her back and leaned over her, his mouth scorching the hollow of her throat and working its way lower. A cold rush of air on Merrie's midriff warned her that, at the same time, Dave was lifting her sweater dangerously high above the waist.

"Enough!" Jerking away, she wiggled out of his embrace and jumped up. "Dave, why don't you go spit tobacco on some mule?"

"I can think of a couple of things I'd rather do." He was already on his feet, advancing toward Merrie. For a split second, she debated standing her ground, then broke and ran for the house.

He launched himself through the kitchen door at her heels, but inside, the advantage belonged to Merrie. She knew the turns and twists intimately, and she also carried a mental map of which spots were habitually occupied by a snoozing cat or pup.

As she raced up the stairs, Merrie could hear Dave muttering an oath at something. Another few steps and she'd be safe in her bedroom . . .

Except that there was no lock on the door.

Merrie swung around at the top of the stairs to confront Dave as he leaped up two steps at a time. "That's enough." Her breath came more rapidly than she would have expected from her brief exertion.

"Really?" Dave paused two steps below the top, his eyes not quite on a level with Merrie's. "That wasn't my impression."

"Dave, I thought we agreed—"

"*You* agreed. Not me." His hand closed over hers on the railing. "This is crazy, Merrie. We belong together."

"No, we don't. That's just the problem." But as his fingers stroked up her arm, Merrie couldn't remember exactly why she'd thought there was a problem.

"We're supposed to be concentrating on the here and now." Dave moved up one step, his body inches from hers.

"But . . ." Merrie's feeble attempt at a protest died in her throat as Dave pinned her arms to her sides and turned her firmly toward the bedroom.

"If you aren't going to get out of my way, I can see I have to take matters into my own hands."

He loomed larger than she remembered, and his arms felt strong and irresistible as he marched her into the bedroom. *I've got to fight this . . .*

But she didn't want to fight nature. Not right now, while Dave was placing her on the bed and pulling off her sneakers. Not while he was kissing her, and she could taste fried chicken and honey on his breath.

Down home. Earlier, Dave had used the words jokingly, but they took on a new meaning to Merrie as she wrapped her arms around him. Home. With Dave, right now, she was home. And to hell with everything else.

His body knew its way this time, and yet there was an edge of newness, too. Their lovemaking was fiercer, more daring, than before. Dave discovered new erotic zones—the inside of Merrie's thigh, the back of her knee, the tip of her left shoulder. And she couldn't get enough of touching him, feeling the hardness and the softness of the man she loved. Yes, loved, however hopeless it might be.

Thoughts wavered, blurred, and vanished into unrestrained sensation as they joined, hip to hip, bone to bone, and heart to heart. Merrie's body demanded, and gave, satisfaction in a way that was new to her. She wanted to ride the earth like a winged horse, to fly through the wind with Dave at her side, to soar and dip and spin.

Too soon, sky and wind met at the far peak of sensation. Floating down afterward, she nestled into a quiet sheltered corner of the universe.

"Again," Dave said.

"I couldn't," she murmured.

Dave began humming the refrain of "My Sweetheart's a Mule."

"How can you be so unromantic at a time like this?" Merrie pulled the handmade quilt over her, as the heat of passion receded.

"How can you be so stubborn?" he countered, burrowing beneath the quilt. "Now let me see . . ."

"Cut it out!" But as his hands and mouth gentled and enflamed her, Merrie no longer wanted him to stop. With a shocking suddenness, her body was no longer her own, but a wild thing at Dave's command. New hungers and longings found expression in her movements as she in turn aroused Dave, delighting in his hoarse gasp as he united them again.

This time there was no wind and no mountains, only Dave and Merrie and the musky scent of lovemaking and the intense pleasure of becoming one with the man she loved. Through spirals of ecstasy, she never lost her awareness that they were right here, right now, and she liked it that way.

If only it could last . . .

"I love you, Merrie." Dave traced one finger over the diamond ring she still wore, as they lay quietly together afterward. "I'm not going to let you go."

"I can't be what you want." She nearly choked on the words, wishing she didn't have to say them.

"Are you still harping on that ridiculous idea?" Dave propped himself up on his elbow. "Merrie, what exactly do you think I expect of you?"

"You tell me." She waited, hoping she would hear something different from what he'd said a week ago, or that he'd express it in some other way that would be less rigid, that she could persuade herself to accept.

"Okay." He rolled back, interlacing his fingers behind his head. "What I want, Merrie, is the woman you really are."

"And who is that?"

"You don't realize your own potential, Merrie." His voice was languid with contentment, or was that smugness? "You have so many talents, so much to offer."

"My guinea pigs like me the way I am." *Please don't say what I think you're going to say.*

"So do I. But I also like what's inside there, what you've been afraid to let out." He reached out and ruffled Merrie's hair. "Do you realize how beautiful you are? Even more than Lizabeth, although you hide it. And there's a natural dignity about you that makes people take notice."

That didn't sound so bad. "Dignity, maybe. But nobody's ever accused me of being graceful."

"That's the point. Your self-image is all screwed up." Dave was just warming up, she saw in dismay. "You hide out as if you didn't deserve better. Look at the way you decorate, with odds and ends that don't even match. And half the time you forget to wear makeup, not that you don't look terrific anyway, but you look even better with it. You need to seek out new friends, people who might challenge you, to socialize more."

"I could be the perfect hostess," Merrie muttered, anger churning inside.

"Yes—"

"Forget it, Dave." Flinging herself out of bed, Merrie began pulling on her clothes. "Look, I'm sorry if that sounded rude, but—" Oh, damn, why did tears have to threaten now? She didn't want to cry! "For your information, those 'odds and ends' I decorate with are handmade artifacts and I love them! I chose them on purpose because they reflect the things that are important to me, like having a real home. Like not having to wear makeup or pick friends who 'challenge' me. This is the way I am, Dave, and if you can't take me, you're going to have to leave me."

Fury darkened Dave's face as he threw back the covers and reached for his own clothes. "You *are* stubborn as a mule, Merrie. Dammit, you misunderstood everything I said."

"I don't think so." *Oh, Dave, I was trying so hard to hear something I could accept. Why did you have to let me down?* "You don't even like the way I live."

He pulled on his sweater. "Forgive me if I insulted your decorating talents, Merrie. That isn't the point."

"The fact that you think I'm upset because you don't like my decorating *is* the point." A rebellious tear freed itself from the corner of her eye, but Merrie did her best to ignore its embarrassing trickle down her cheek. "Dave, I'm not a hostess, and I'm not a raving beauty. I spent a year in New York wearing makeup and 'fulfilling my potential,' and it's for the birds."

"I think you've got me mixed up with that guy who didn't like children and animals."

"No." Another tear broke loose, wending its way across her cheek to one ear. "You've got so many of the qualities I'm looking for, Dave. So many things that I love. But you can't accept me as I am."

"Do you realize how adolescent that sounds?"

"You arrogant—" She broke off, not wanting to say things she would regret. "Dave, I think you'd better go."

He hesitated, then nodded. "We'll talk this out when you're calmer."

"When *I'm* calmer?" The more they argued, the angrier she got. "Dave, I just wish you could hear yourself through my ears!"

"So do I." He paused in the doorway, his face a mask of frustration. "Dammit, Merrie, maybe then I could see a way to convince you how unreasonable you're being." They stared at each other, anguished, and then he walked out the door, stalking heavily down the stairs. Merrie stood where she was, her chest swelling with the ache of needing him, until she heard the front door close below.

She blinked and let the tears cascade down. Darn it, she had a right to cry. She might never lie in Dave's arms again, and she missed him already.

CHAPTER
Twelve

WHENEVER MERRIE SAW DAVE that week during the wedding preparations, the two of them greeted each other with a touch of constraint. But where she felt tense and awkward, Dave appeared unfazed by their falling out.

It hurt to see him smile and joke with Drum and Lizabeth as if nothing were wrong. Merrie herself tried to keep up a cheerful façade, of course, but she didn't feel as if Dave was pretending.

He thinks I'm going to come around. The realization angered her, tempering her anguish—but only a little.

Friday, the night before the wedding, the rehearsal went smoothly, even though Steffie was overexcited and kept skipping off to investigate some new discovery in the hotel ballroom. Drum showed remarkable patience with her, even when Lizabeth's temper was near snapping.

"She'll be fine tomorrow," he assured his bride-to-be, who was fidgeting as Drum shepherded the child back into the aisle between rows of portable molded seats.

"I certainly hope so," Lizabeth muttered, and rolled her eyes for Merrie's benefit.

Dave had come directly from work. In his three-piece suit, he exuded confidence. *The man who always gets his way. But not this time.* Still, Merrie couldn't

dispel the memory of last weekend, of the joy she'd
known in his arms. Wasn't there some way they could
work it out?

Only if he were willing to meet her halfway. And so
far he hadn't even acknowledged that he needed to
compromise.

After the rehearsal, they adjourned to Sarah's condominium, where she was having the rehearsal dinner catered, graciously standing in for the groom's absent
parents. The condominium, on Nashville's fashionable
west side, was a spacious, modern structure, the living
room featuring a cathedral ceiling. Three small round
tables had been set up in the living room, and the
shrimp cocktail was already in place when Merrie and
Netta arrived in the station wagon.

While Sarah supervised the caterers' assistants, Gigi
held court on the sofa. The mother of the bride was
recounting a lively story of madcap doings on the Riviera, to the obvious amusement of Drum's sister
Frances, a rather matronly, pleasant woman who had
arrived that morning as the family's representative.
Gigi's hair was a shade too red, her face too wrinkle-
free to be the untouched work of nature, and yet the
word that best described her at this moment was . . .
charming.

Merrie glanced up, to see Sarah Anders standing in
the kitchen doorway regarding Gigi with a mild frown.
It struck Merrie that, if she *did* marry Dave, her own
rehearsal dinner would be exactly like this—meticulous
and lovely, except for the fact that her mother-in-law
would most likely prefer that the mother of the bride
had stayed on the other side of the globe.

"Time to eat," Sarah called, and Merrie found her
place card at a table with Drum and Frances. Lizabeth
and Netta shared one of the ice-cream-style tables with

Sarah, while Dave was already pretending to flirt with his companions, Gigi and Steffie.

At first, the conversation at Merrie's table covered general topics—Nashville's building boom, the new hotel, the rehearsal earlier that evening—but after a while Drum and Frances stopped acting like polite strangers and got down to being brother and sister.

"I hope Merrie doesn't mind if we talk family." Frances set aside her knife and fork, leaving her *boeuf bourguignon* only half-eaten. "Drum, you know Mum and Dad would have loved to be here, but with only two weeks' notice, they simply couldn't."

"Why pretend?" Drum didn't sound angry, only resigned. "Look, Fran, I appreciate your coming. I just want you to tell the others that this marriage is going to be a lot happier than the last one."

"Nancy Ann was a classmate of mine at Vassar," Frances explained to Merrie. "I suppose it's my fault for introducing them, but she seemed perfect."

Drum's mouth twisted with irony, but he busied himself with his stuffed potato and kept silent.

"She's never remarried, and I suppose the family was hoping for a reconciliation." Apparently realizing her words might be misinterpreted, Frances added quickly, "That was before they met Lizabeth, of course."

"I don't want to darken the evening by talking about the past, but I'd like you both to know one thing about Nancy Ann." Drum set his crystal glass firmly on the tablecloth. "When I called her to ask if Drum the Fourth and Nan—my kids—could come for the wedding, she refused. She said it wasn't part of our visitation agreement, and I'd have to go to court. Which she knew was impossible. I telephoned them both at school, and Nan was crying, she wanted so much to be here."

It was the longest speech Merrie had heard Drum

make, and her heart squeezed at his obvious distress. This was a man who loved his children deeply.

"When will you see them again?" she asked.

"I get them for a month in the summer and for Thanksgiving. Isn't that rich? Not even Christmas." Then Drum's tone softened. "I've been thinking—Steffie's old enough to enjoy Disney World, isn't she? Maybe we can take the three of them to Florida in July. My kids are really excited about having a little sister."

"I'm sure Steffie would love it." Merrie's enthusiasm was genuine. No need to worry about Drum and his new daughter; it might take them a while to get to know each other, but they'd be just fine.

After the last *crème caramel* had been consumed, the dinner broke up, everyone wanting to get a good night's rest before the wedding. Dave said good night to Merrie in front of the others, with a quick kiss. "By the time it's our turn, we'll be old hands at weddings," he teased, to the obvious approval of everyone except Merrie.

Her cheeks burned as she walked out to the car. When she and Netta were finally on their way, Merrie said, "He's made up his mind we're going to get married."

"So I see."

"You think it's a good idea." Merrie didn't need to ask; she knew her grandmother well enough to guess the answer. "But he wants it on his terms. His house, his lifestyle. He wants me to 'fulfill my potential.'"

"I take it you've tried talking to him about it." Netta tugged on her gloves. The car heater was being cranky again, issuing occasional gusts of heat followed by blasts of chilly air.

"I don't think he really hears me." Merrie gritted her teeth, staring at the roadway ahead. "I can't seem to get through to him that this isn't some superficial thing. Do you know what he said? He accused me of decorating with odds and ends!"

"Well, it isn't formal like his house. But I'd hardly call it odds and ends." Netta stared out the window, deep in thought, before adding, "It reminds me of an old story."

"I'm game." Merrie paused at a red light.

"A farmer wasn't having any luck training his mule, so he hired a mule-trainer. The man pulled out a board and began hitting the mule over the head. The farmer protested, 'I hired you to train him, not to kill him!' And the trainer replied, 'Sure, but I've got to get his attention first.'"

Merrie burst out laughing. "Got any spare boards lying around?"

"You'll think of something," was her grandmother's response.

As she changed for bed that night, Merrie remembered that Dave had teasingly referred to *her* as a mule, in one of his folk songs. *It looks like the shoe is on the other hoof this time.*

Although she lay awake for more than an hour, no brilliant ideas came to her for getting Dave's attention.

"Are the guests arriving already?" Lizabeth, ready except for her gown, sat before the mirror in the suite she and Drum shared. Chased out by his future sister-in-law and mother-in-law, he'd gone downstairs to have a drink with Dave.

"Starting to trickle in," Gigi agreed. "Having the hotel staff at our disposal is *très* convenient, *n'est-ce pas?*" The mother of the bride had chosen a conservative lavender suit, no doubt at Lizabeth's instigation. "I saw a couple of your friends, Liz, and that lady from the modeling agency. Imagine, coming all the way to Nashville on such short notice!"

"Keep an eye on things for me downstairs, will you, Mother?" Lizabeth fluffed up the mass of ringlets created earlier by the hotel's coiffeur to set off the bridal hat. "Merrie can help me finish up here."

Gigi was obviously eager to be where the action was. "Well, I don't mind. I'll just go back down and greet people."

"And make sure Netta doesn't let Steffie rumple her dress!" Lizabeth called as her mother went out the door.

"She's in her glory today." Merrie slipped on her bridesmaid's gown, turning so Lizabeth could zip it up the back.

"I know, but . . . well, she's so antsy, she was making me nervous." Lizabeth turned Merrie around again to look at her. "Terrific. My little sister. Who'd have thought we'd both have such good luck?"

"You look stunning, even without your dress." Merrie began brushing out her short locks.

"You like it?" Lizabeth twirled in her slip. "Maybe I should go down the aisle this way. Think how disappointed Drum's folks would be that they missed it!"

The sisters giggled together.

"But seriously, folks." Lizabeth removed her white gown from the hanger and handed it to Merrie. "You know, I'm glad we've had these last two weeks to get to know each other better. Before, I thought of you as sort of a rebel. I mean, I knew it took hard work to become a veterinarian, but, well, it felt like you were doing it just to spite us."

"I suppose it must have been hard to see why anyone would give up all that glamour in New York." Merrie held the dress out so her sister could step into it. "But for me, it wore thin pretty quickly."

"Sometimes"—Lizabeth wiggled her arms into the sleeves—"sometimes it's beginning to wear thin for me, too. That's one reason I was so delighted to find Drum, to move on to a new phase in my life. But I don't need to tell you about that, do I?"

Merrie fastened the hooks and eyes that closed the dress, afraid to respond.

"I don't suppose getting married will change you all that much, though." Lizabeth tilted her head, reflecting. "There's a down-to-earth quality about you that I never appreciated before. I think you get it from Grandma Netta. You can be a lady with the best of them, but you never forget what's really important."

"Like Steffie," Merrie blurted without thinking. "I mean, we both think she's important, don't we?"

Lizabeth began fastening her hat into place atop the curls. "Do you think I'm a horrible mother? I know I'm flighty, Merrie. But I do love my little girl."

"I know. And so does Drum." Merrie could still see the glow on his face as he'd talked about taking the children to Disney World.

"And Dave," Lizabeth added. "You're lucky, my dear. Men like that are hard to find, and harder to keep."

Merrie didn't know how to answer her, so she said nothing.

For once, Lizabeth was attuned to her sister's mood rather than wrapped up in her own thoughts, and she didn't miss the significance of Merrie's silence. "You know, I thought you two looked a little strained at dinner last night. Is anything wrong?"

"There are some issues we haven't resolved yet." Merrie averted her face on the pretext of applying more lipstick. "Liz, if we didn't get married, would you— would you still let Steffie stay with me?"

She heard her sister take a deep breath. "Are you saying you'd actually marry the man just to get Steffie?"

"Not exactly." Merrie blotted the lipstick on a tissue. "I don't think I'd go that far."

When she looked up, her sister was staring at her with realization dawning in those bright blue eyes. "But you'd get engaged for that reason, wouldn't you?"

Merrie felt like a general who'd won a series of battles, only to lose the war when she inadvertently betrayed her own troops. There was no use denying the truth; her sister would only see through her. "Oh, Liz. I'm sorry. You were goading me about not being able to please a man, and I was sort of teasing you, and then before I knew it, I'd gone too far to back out."

She wanted to argue further, but instinct told her that doing so wouldn't help matters. Instead, she waited in anguish for Lizabeth's response.

The hat brim hid the bride's face as she anchored the crown with a long, jeweled pin. Then her shoulders began to shake.

"Are you all right?" Merrie caught her sister to steady her, then realized that Lizabeth was laughing.

"The whole engagement party—that was to impress us? Just so you could get Steffie? Oh, lordie! You can't tell me Sarah Anders knew about that!"

"No," Merrie admitted.

"Oh, that's right!" Lizabeth stopped giggling and stared at her own mirrored reflection in dismay. "I'm the one who told her, at the restaurant! Oh, you must have been furious! And Dave just went right along with it. Why, that sly fox! He intends to marry you, whether you like it or not."

"That's the problem," Merrie conceded. "He's so— arrogant. But that's between him and me. Liz, are you angry?"

"No. But we'd better not tell Drum. His sense of humor isn't his strong point." Lizabeth was still grinning as she turned to meet Merrie's gaze. "After spending the last few weeks here, I've come to the conclusion that when Steffie can't be with us, she belongs in Nashville with people who love her. And that includes you, honey, whether you marry Dave or not. Although I have a feeling you will."

"Oh, Liz!" Merrie could barely restrain herself from hugging her sister and wrinkling both their dresses. "I'm so glad."

A light tap at the door was followed by Gigi's eager face. "Aren't you two ready? Everybody's here, positively everybody!"

"We'll be right down," Lizabeth promised as their mother departed.

Merrie darted into the adjoining room, which was hers for the day, and rummaged in her suitcase. On Lizabeth's instructions, she'd brought along her swimsuit and racquetball gear in case she wanted to work out in the hotel's facilities later. Finally, at the bottom, she found an old-fashioned lace garter worked with blue ribbon.

"Here, slip this on." She returned with it quickly. "Something old, something new, something borrowed, and something blue, remember?"

"It's both blue and borrowed." Lizabeth nodded approval as she pulled the garter over her stocking and stepped into her white-on-white embroidered shoes. "And at thirty-one, I guess I qualify as old for a bride, and everything else is new, so we're all set. The garter's the perfect finishing touch."

"I bought it at a handicrafts show last week." Merrie stood back and surveyed her sister. "You look gorgeous."

"Wish me luck." Lizabeth leaned forward for a kiss, then snatched up her bouquet of white roses and baby's breath. "Let's go, now!"

They hurried downstairs together. Lizabeth and Drum were to walk down the aisle together, and he was waiting by the bank of elevators to claim his bride as she emerged. Merrie was the only other witness to the pure love that illuminated his face as he caught sight of Lizabeth.

Merrie ducked past the two lovers, hurrying to take her place outside the ballroom and listen for her cue in the organ music. Her heart thundered with happiness and pain, relief and longing, and, undeniably, envy. If only it were Dave, looking at her that way. Loving her unreservedly instead of wanting to make her over in his own image.

Beside her in the hallway, Netta restrained a high-spirited Steffie, who hopped from one foot to the other, each jolt threatening to dislodge the rose petals from her basket. Finally, Netta urged the child forward, and Steffie half-skipped down the aisle, flinging the petals about with wild abandon.

The music changed, and Merrie glided with measured tread down the aisle. Around her, she heard the buzz of conversation die down. There seemed to be a lot of people filling the rows of seats, but she couldn't pick out any faces, only the one waiting at the end of the aisle near the minister. Dave, the best man, elegant in a black-and-white tuxedo, stood watching her approach and smiling with proud appreciation.

It was all Merrie could do not to walk right to his side and link her arm through his. Dammit, they *did* belong together—the real Merrie and the real Dave— not some pair of society bookends. She wanted to snuggle up with him in a rumpled bed in a comfortable house full of animals and kids, where no decorator ever dared set foot except as a guest. And she wanted to lead a life full of quirks and playfulness, love and snowmen and Santa Claus suits.

Somehow Merrie steered herself into her assigned place beside Steffie and turned to watch her sister and Drum sail joyously down the aisle.

Surely everyone present could feel the magic that surrounded these two lovers. It seemed to Merrie that she had never before truly understood the full significance of marriage, the almost supernatural bond that was woven with the exchange of vows and hearts for a lifetime. In a daze, she heard the words of the ceremony, watched the ring being slipped onto Lizabeth's finger and saw Drum lean forward for his kiss. The hat brim bumped his forehead, and he chuckled along with some of the guests as he pushed it back and embraced his bride.

Then Lizabeth and Drum were gone, an enchanted pair vanishing up the aisle, as Dave extended his arm for Merrie and they followed, with Steffie close behind.

Merrie blinked away tears she hadn't even known were there. Dave halted outside the ballroom, as if to speak with her, but they were instantly engulfed by well-wishers. Then Gigi came to fetch them for the receiving line in the adjacent Gold Room, where the hotel staff had set out a sumptuous luncheon and a many-tiered white cake.

The next hour was a blur of faces, handshakes, and repeated murmurings of "thank you" to all the congratulations. Merrie's feet hurt, and her stomach was growling by the time the line broke up. She ducked away as Dave approached, and saw him shrug and turn to talk with Drum.

She couldn't face him right now. She might give in,

agree to a future she knew wouldn't work. It hurt, to know they'd come this close to happiness but could never go those last few yards, the ones Lizabeth and Drum had traveled so lightly today. And she loved Dave so much, she didn't know how she could bear to live apart from him.

Merrie could only sample the crab-stuffed mushrooms, lobster tails, and fresh asparagus, her usually robust appetite deserting her. She ached to slip away, perhaps to work out in the swimming pool, but duty required that she stay to the end. Dave, on the other hand, appeared to be enjoying his role of best man, beaming as he made the rounds of the guests.

He really did enjoy being part of society. It wasn't an affectation. The realization didn't comfort Merrie in the slightest.

Calls of "There they are!" roused her, and she turned to see Drum and Lizabeth in the doorway, changed into the clothes they would wear on the honeymoon flight to Fiji.

"Come on!" Lizabeth was signaling to Merrie and a couple of other young women, who trailed after her to the hotel's grand staircase. There, the bride skipped up the steps until she could fling her bouquet into their midst.

Merrie reached up automatically, not making much effort to catch it, but Lizabeth had aimed the bouquet well, and it fell into Merrie's arms. The other women chuckled and teased her as they hurried out to watch Lizabeth and Drum depart in a limousine.

Steffie was yawning, and Grandma Netta clucked at her. "We're going up to your room for a nap," she announced, and the child was so exhausted she went without a protest.

Not sure whether her duties as maid of honor were

finally over, Merrie wandered back toward the ballroom. Frances stopped her in the hall outside.

"I just wanted you to know that I'm delighted." Drum's sister spoke with a patrician Boston accent, but her words were frank and open. "My parents have some silly rules, although they'd never admit it, about who's 'one of us,' and so forth. But I've never seen my brother so happy, and I'm glad he found your sister."

In spite of her own tangled thoughts, Merrie smiled. "I don't know what the etiquette books say, Frances, but I consider you my sister-in-law."

"I'm honored." Frances gave her a hug. "And if you ever come up to Boston, I'd love for you to be my houseguest."

"I'd like that."

"Oh, I nearly forgot." Frances paused as she turned to go. "Dave said he'll be down in the racquetball court, in case you're looking for a game."

"Thanks." They exchanged good-byes, and then Merrie went into the ballroom for a last look around.

The crowd was thinning out, although the hotel staff still kept the hot trays full. In one corner, Merrie was startled to see her mother and Sarah Anders sitting at a table together, sipping their champagne. Gigi had kicked off her heels, and her stockinged feet rested boldly on one of the chairs.

Sarah looked relaxed and not at all offended by the discarded shoes, although she herself sat properly in her chair. As Merrie stood there debating whether to go over to them, she overheard snippets of their conversation.

"Two daughters, and both marrying well." Gigi's words made her daughter cringe, but Sarah didn't bat an eyelash; perhaps she believed Gigi was referring to her son's personality, rather than to his fortune. And perhaps she was right.

Merrie was momentarily distracted as a waitress offered her some hors d'oeuvres, and then she heard her mother say, "You know, Sally—do you mind if I call you that?—I always envied you."

"Whatever for?" Sarah patted back a wilting wing of hair above her temple.

"Class." A world of envy was packed into that word. "You've got it, *chèrie*, without even trying. Always did. The real stuff. I couldn't get that kind of class even if I married a prince. Look at me." Gigi made a champagne-wobbly gesture that took in her own appearance. "Oh, I don't look so bad today, but I do things wrong. I know that—I always go for colors that are too bright, dresses that knock your eye out. *Ce n'est pas classique, tu comprends?*"

"Oh, Georgia." Sarah shook her head. "How *I* used to envy *you.*"

"You did?" Gigi sat up straighter, so startled that her always-uncertain French accent skidded into an unmistakable Tennessee twang. "You've got to be putting me on!"

"I've never told this to anyone." Sarah lowered her voice, and Merrie hesitated. She hadn't meant to eavesdrop, and she certainly didn't want to sneak closer, even though neither of the women was taking any notice of her. But somehow she couldn't help wandering toward the refreshment table and pausing so that Sarah's words were slightly more audible.

"I always wished I had your spontaneity," Dave's mother was saying. "You're not afraid of anything. I loved my husband, and I don't mind the trappings of society, but . . . I never had a chance to find out who I really was. I suppose it's my own fault. I try to tell myself that thirty-five years ago women just weren't as free as they are today, but you didn't let that stop *you*."

The rest of her words were lost on Merrie. It struck her for the first time that someday she, too, might be looking back on her life, thirty-five years from now. What would she be thinking? It was hard to imagine herself that much older. Would she be drinking champagne at her daughter's wedding? Or would she ever have children, ever marry? How could she love anyone else as much as she loved Dave?

I don't want to look back at my life and regret the opportunities I let pass me by.

Dave. Dammit, she loved him, and he loved her. Why should his stiff-necked arrogance stand in their way? Grandma Netta had said you had to get a mule's attention before you could teach him anything. Well, it was worth a try.

With that thought in mind, Merrie swept upstairs to change into her racquetball clothes.

CHAPTER
Thirteen

MERRIE PAUSED IN THE observation room overhead to watch Dave play before revealing her presence. Even through the glass, she could hear the squeal and thump of the ball as it smashed off the front wall of the court. Dave caught his own shot without difficulty, banking it off both walls and sending it back to himself at a sharp angle. He leaped for it, and missed.

He plays well, but he's distracted. Well, darn it, so am I.

She padded down the stairs to the court level, acutely conscious of the skimpiness of her costume. The red jogging shorts and red, white, and blue T-shirt had seemed perfectly sensible when she was playing with Sue Brown, but now Merrie realized that her arms and legs were bare, and the T-shirt did nothing to hide the curves of her body.

Oh, well, Dave had seen a lot more than that. She just didn't want either of them to get sidetracked right now.

Listening to make sure she wasn't walking into the path of a ball traveling at a hundred miles per hour, Merrie opened the door to the court. "Hi. Frances said I'd find you here."

Dave was standing between the service lines, and at her voice he turned and smiled. "I was hoping you'd join me."

Up close, his skin had a burnished sheen from his exertions, and his crisp tennis whites highlighted the muscular hardness of his body. Merrie planted herself at the back of the court, unwilling to come any closer.

"I'll take a handicap, if you want to play." Absently, Dave adjusted the glove on his right hand, which kept the racquet from slipping. His eyes never left Merrie's face.

"Why don't we just hit it around a little? I feel like talking, not keeping score." *Besides this is one contest I want us both to win.*

"Okay by me." Lifting his racquet, Dave smashed the ball into the front wall with a popping crack. It caromed off, and Merrie caught it on the fly, smacking it into a corner so it deflected at an odd angle, and Dave missed it.

"Not bad," he said.

"For a woman?" she teased as she retrieved the ball.

Dave stepped back, yielding the service lines. "Hey, I didn't say that. But you have to admit, this is a game of power."

"And strategy." Merrie returned his gaze directly. "I suppose the stronger player has the advantage, but the craftier one can hold her own."

"No argument there."

For a while, they volleyed and chased the ball around the court, trading the serve back and forth. The game was fast and challenging, which was why Merrie liked it, and although her arm began to ache from returning Dave's high-powered strokes, she was pleased to see she was more or less keeping up with him.

"Good reflexes," he observed as one of her returns eluded him.

"It's all in the footwork." She collected the ball and headed for the service lines again.

As she loped forward, Merrie realized what was different about this court from the ones she was used to. The white cement walls were pristine and new, not stained with blue-gray at shoulder-height from the impact of the blue racquetball. And there were none of the usual background noises, the shouts of players and crack of shots she always heard at the health club. She and Dave were alone here.

Instead of serving, she turned around. "Dave, I really came down here to talk."

"Time out," he agreed, swinging his racquet slightly as he strolled toward her.

"I've been thinking about things." Setting her racquet on the floor, Merrie massaged the sore muscles in her right arm. "I heard our mothers reminiscing, and I started wondering how I'd feel, looking back when I'm their age."

"Good. Because frankly, I was hoping today would generate a little enthusiasm for planning our own wedding." He certainly didn't beat around the bush.

"In a way it did." *Shock him, Merrie; get his attention.* "I'm willing to marry you, but only on my terms."

"And they are?"

He was standing a few feet away, but Merrie felt engulfed by him. It took all her determination to stand her ground. "First of all, we live in *my* house." Seeing that he was about to object, she hurried on. "The only parties we'll give are the potluck, come-as-you-are kind. And I'd like you to develop your gift for guitar playing. Not that I expect you to give up your career, of course, but I want you to develop your full potential. My dad was a musician, after all, and we have a family tradition to uphold."

The puzzled expression on his face was so droll, Merrie had a hard time restraining nervous laughter.

Quickly, she tried to think of some more conditions to make her point. "Of course, if you do need to entertain formally once in a while, you have that nice car to do it in. I don't mind if you hire a caterer to pass the hors d'oeuvres around while you give your guests a tour of Nashville."

Dave chuckled. "Is this a joke?"

"Oh, no. I'm perfectly serious." Merrie bent down to retrieve her racquet. "That's it. We can play some more now, if you want."

"All right." Still wearing a bemused expression, he moved back as Merrie served. They volleyed for a while until he missed, and she served again. This time she lost the point, and they exchanged places.

"What was all that about, anyway?" he asked as they passed each other.

"Think about it," Merrie said.

The intensity of the game, coupled with her own tension, was wearing down her endurance, and Merrie lost the next few points.

"Want to pack it in?" Dave eyed her with concern. "You're beginning to wilt."

"I suppose." She waited for him to say something more about her preposterous demands, but he didn't. Merrie's shoulders sagged as she walked off the court. She hadn't made the point she'd intended.

"Want to try the hot tub?" Dave caught up with her.

"I left my swimsuit upstairs."

"There's no one here." He peered around mischievously at the empty spa facilities.

Any other time, Merrie might have been tempted, but not today. There was too much on her mind—like her entire future happiness. "Dave, look, about our engagement. I told Lizabeth the truth, and she's still going to let Steffie stay with me. So maybe we can wait a week or so and then call the whole thing off, okay?"

All trace of amusement vanished from his face as he caught Merrie's shoulders and spun her toward him, anger darkening his gray eyes. "We're not going one step further until you explain to me what this is all about. First you say some absurd things about entertaining in my car, and now you're trying to walk out of my life. Well, I'm not going to let you, Merrie."

Her throat clogged with tears. "Dave, can't you see how hopeless it is?"

"All I see is two people in love with each other, and one of them is stubborn as a mule."

"And that one is you." A sudden fury cut through her misery. "You think what I was asking is ridiculous? What about what you want me to do? Give up my house, move into that hotel you call a home, fulfill my 'true potential' by mincing around playing hostess? That's no more sensible than expecting you to serve hors d'oeuvres in your car!"

"Oh, so that's what you were getting at." Dave shook his head. "Merrie, this is all so unimportant. We'll work it out after we get married."

"We'll work it out first or we're not getting married." She glared at him, her fists clenched in frustration. "Don't you see how patronizing that was, telling me that my hidden potential is to look like a model and bring compliments from your friends? That's the same side of me Franco wanted, the pretty girl he could show off."

"I'm not Franco." With a tenderness that nearly unnerved her, Dave brushed a wisp of damp hair off Merrie's forehead. "I'm sorry if it sounded like I wanted the same thing he did, but it's not true."

"Are you willing to give up your lifestyle and come live my way?" Merrie demanded.

"That's excessive." A note of irritation underlay Dave's obvious attempt to sound patient and reasonable.

"I agree," Merrie said.

"You do?"

"I agree that it's excessive to expect me to give up my lifestyle and come live your way," she snapped. "It shows a selfish attitude and a lack of respect for me as a person."

To her surprise, Dave threw back his head and laughed. "Oh, Merrie, you really put me in my place! 'A selfish attitude and a lack of respect.' Wow. Who is that guy? I don't think I like him. Here he finds himself a terrific lady like you, and then he acts like a jerk."

"Are you laughing at me?" She was so angry she wanted to smash her racquet over his head.

"Not exactly." Apparently noting the way her hand was tightening on the racquet, he ducked away in mock fear. "Maybe at myself. I do have a pompous side, don't I?"

"Really? I hadn't noticed." Merrie felt her wrath begin to melt into the glimmerings of mirth. Dave looked so warm and comical, pretending to cower away from her. "Well? Are you going to accept my terms?"

"Can I buy one of those cars with a bar?" He remained just outside the range of her racquet as he led the way to the elevators. "I mean, if that's where I'm going to be entertaining."

"It's your car. I wouldn't dream of interfering." She shrugged. "Hire a chauffeur; I don't care. But if he tries to pass a single tray of anything around my living room, you're out, both of you!"

"You drive a hard bargain." As the elevator doors opened, Dave dodged inside as if he were being attacked. Merrie followed at a more dignified pace, willing to play along but first wanting to be sure he was taking her seriously.

"You'd really live in my house?" she asked as the doors shut the two of them in together.

"'Whither thou goest,' etc., etc." Without warning, Dave pinned her against the side of the elevator. He smelled rich and earthy after his workout on the court, and Merrie found herself responding to his embrace with a sudden surge of longing. Her mouth opened before his silent demand, and her arms claimed him even as he drew her close. Vaguely, she was aware of the elevator's rise, and wondered if someone might interrupt them; but then, there was hardly anybody in the hotel.

"Your place or mine?" he murmured as the lift glided to a halt.

"What floor are we on?" Merrie asked.

She felt Dave turn to examine the display. "Ten."

"My place," she said.

They moved through the lushly carpeted hallway to Merrie's room. No sooner had she fitted the key into the lock than she felt herself lifted off her feet. Dave cradled her in his arms as he stepped over the threshold.

"What on earth are you doing?" Merrie demanded.

"Rehearsing." He kicked the door shut and deposited her on the king-size bed. "For our honeymoon."

"I take it that wasn't the only rehearsing you had in mind," she murmured as he knelt to kiss the pulse of her throat, his hands exploring her breasts through the thin T-shirt.

"Practice makes perfect."

Merrie lost all interest in words as he aroused her in his own expert way. This was a game to put all others in the shade: fast and eager, volley answering volley, the heat mounting, her breath coming fast, all senses honed to a new level of awareness. They were not competitors but partners, triumphing together, a matched pair, moving faster and faster until Merrie lost all control, all conscious thought, crying and laughing and holding on to Dave as hard as she could.

"My God, I love you, woman." His voice still rough with passion, Dave lay beside her tracing the curve of Merrie's temple. "I'd live with you in a cave if that's what you wanted."

"No, thanks," she murmured sleepily. "It wouldn't be comfortable for Steffie."

Although she was about to doze off, Dave didn't sound tired at all. "What did Lizabeth say?"

"About what?"

"About our charade."

"Oh." Merrie yawned. "She thought it was funny. And she said you were going to marry me anyway."

"She was right." He nuzzled the curve of her neck, just below the jaw. "Hey, this may sound impertinent at a time like this, but I'm hungry."

And so was she, Merrie realized with a start. She'd hardly eaten at the reception, and she'd certainly exerted herself this afternoon. A glance at her watch on the bed-table showed that it was after six o'clock.

"Do you suppose room service is open yet?" she asked.

"I doubt it." At his prodding, Merrie finally gave up the idea of taking a nap, and they arose and showered together. She dressed and packed up her gear in the suitcase, since she was planning to return home tonight.

"Do you suppose Netta and Steffie are still here?" Dave asked as they adjourned to his room on the floor below, where he changed into street clothes.

"Oh! I forgot about them! Yes, they were going to take a nap, and I'm sure they'd call me before they left." Merrie stared at herself guiltily in Dave's mirror, wondering if others would be able to detect the new glow of happiness in her cheeks. Was it possible that Dave really had agreed to meet her halfway? She supposed it would take days or weeks to get used to the idea. But she was in no hurry; joy was something to be savored, not rushed.

As they returned to the elevator, Merrie's thoughts were already flying ahead, to that not-so-distant time when Dave would be her husband. Now that he'd agreed to live her way, in her house, a few second thoughts began creeping in.

"Dave?" She watched the lighted numbers descend on the display above the elevator doors. "Is it going to make problems for you? Not being able to entertain formally, I mean?"

"You mean will the boss fire me? I doubt it." He grinned. "Since I'm the boss."

"Yes, but—"

"Feeling guilty?" he teased, then sobered as he saw that her concern was genuine. "Merrie, I can always rent a hotel ballroom, or a room in a restaurant. And I suspect most of my friends would enjoy a backyard barbecue as much as a cocktail party. Maybe more."

"But it seemed so important to you." They'd reached the second floor, where Netta and Steffie were lodged, and stood talking in the hallway.

"I won't pretend I don't like a touch of glamour now and then." Dave toyed with Merrie's hand, his finger tracing the antique diamonds of the engagement ring. "I hope you won't mind if we go to the symphony once in a while; maybe even a theater trip to New York or London. You really are a stunning woman; a man couldn't help wanting to show you off. But what's really important will be the home we make together, where we can kick our shoes off and be ourselves. Or Sherlock Holmes and Dr. Watson."

"Or Santa and one of his elves," Merrie couldn't resist adding. "Steffie's going to get wise to old St. Nick one of these days. Maybe she can become the littlest elf at Christmas parties."

"A family tradition." Dave tucked her hand through the crook of his arm. "Now, I think we should celebrate the start of our *real* engagement with a formal dinner tonight."

Merrie hesitated. "I thought we were going to eat with Steffie and Netta." *Are we going to have a disagreement already?*

"Absolutely." Dave strolled beside her toward Netta's room. "I suggest we have a pizza and antipasto salad catered in your living room, by candlelight. Enough to feed three grown-ups, one five-year-old, and —how many cats and dogs and guinea pigs?"

"As many as we can squeeze in," Merrie said happily and pulled him forward as she skipped down the hotel corridor eager to meet the future.

Second Chance At Love

COMING NEXT MONTH

RAINBOW'S END #436
by Carole Buck
When widowed mom Pat Webster
wins a free membership in a posh health
club, the club's owner, dashing Mike Taylor,
falls in love with her. Pat and Mike
share a passion for running—
and for each other...

TEMPTRESS #437
by Linda Raye
Amanda Brady plays a temptress
on TV, so her new brother-in-law, history
professor Nick Logan, assumes she's
a lipstick-brained sexpot. Vowing revenge,
Amanda enrolls in Nick's class, but
teacher and pupil learn unanticipated
lessons in love...

Second Chance At Love

Be Sure to Read These New Releases!

A LADY'S CHOICE #432
by Cait Logan

Emily Northrup returns to her
rural hometown to nurse an ailing aunt
and clashes with her aunt's sexy neighbor,
Cal McDonald. Cal's fascinated Emily
since her teen-age years, and their passion
explodes as the townspeople place
bets on their wedding date...

CLOSE SCRUTINY #433
by Pat Dalton

F.B.I. agent Niera Pascotti
has lived dangerously while loving
cautiously—until a mandatory vacation
to Tahiti throws her into the arms of
mysterious Cort Tucker. Niera can't resist
Cort, yet she must discover his identity
while masking her own...

SECOND CHANCE AT LOVE

___ 0-425-10048-0	IN NAME ONLY #400 Mary Modean	$2.25
___ 0-425-10049-9	RECLAIM THE DREAM #401 Liz Grady	$2.25
___ 0-425-10050-2	CAROLINA MOON #402 Joan Darling	$2.25
___ 0-425-10051-0	THE WEDDING BELLE #403 Diana Morgan	$2.25
___ 0-425-10052-9	COURTING TROUBLE #404 Laine Allen	$2.25
___ 0-425-10053-7	EVERYBODY'S HERO #405 Jan Mathews	$2.25
___ 0-425-10080-4	CONSPIRACY OF HEARTS #406 Pat Dalton	$2.25
___ 0-425-10081-2	HEAT WAVE #407 Lee Williams	$2.25
___ 0-425-10082-0	TEMPORARY ANGEL #408 Courtney Ryan	$2.25
___ 0-425-10083-9	HERO AT LARGE #409 Steffie Hall	$2.25
___ 0-425-10084-7	CHASING RAINBOWS #410 Carole Buck	$2.25
___ 0-425-10085-5	PRIMITIVE GLORY #411 Cass McAndrew	$2.25
___ 0-425-10225-4	TWO'S COMPANY #412 Sherryl Woods	$2.25
___ 0-425-10226-2	WINTER FLAME #413 Kelly Adams	$2.25
___ 0-425-10227-0	A SWEET TALKIN' MAN #414 Jackie Leigh	$2.25
___ 0-425-10228-9	TOUCH OF MIDNIGHT #415 Kerry Price	$2.25
___ 0-425-10229-7	HART'S DESIRE #416 Linda Raye	$2.25
___ 0-425-10230-0	A FAMILY AFFAIR #417 Cindy Victor	$2.25
___ 0-425-10513-X	CUPID'S CAMPAIGN #418 Kate Gilbert	$2.50
___ 0-425-10514-8	GAMBLER'S LADY #419 Cait Logan	$2.50
___ 0-425-10515-6	ACCENT ON DESIRE #420 Christa Merlin	$2.50
___ 0-425-10516-4	YOUNG AT HEART #421 Jackie Leigh	$2.50
___ 0-425-10517-2	STRANGER FROM THE PAST #422 Jan Mathews	$2.50
___ 0-425-10518-0	HEAVEN SENT #423 Jamisan Whitney	$2.50
___ 0-425-10530-X	ALL THAT JAZZ #424 Carole Buck	$2.50
___ 0-425-10531-8	IT STARTED WITH A KISS #425 Kit Windham	$2.50
___ 0-425-10558-X	ONE FROM THE HEART #426 Cinda Richards	$2.50
___ 0-425-10559-8	NIGHTS IN SHINING SPLENDOR #427 Christina Dair	$2.50
___ 0-425-10560-1	ANGEL ON MY SHOULDER #428 Jackie Leigh	$2.50
___ 0-425-10561-X	RULES OF THE HEART #429 Samantha Quinn	$2.50
___ 0-425-10604-7	PRINCE CHARMING REPLIES #430 Sherryl Woods	$2.50
___ 0-425-10605-5	DESIRE'S DESTINY #431 Jamisan Whitney	$2.50
___ 0-425-10680-2	A LADY'S CHOICE #432 Cait Logan	$2.50
___ 0-425-10681-0	CLOSE SCRUTINY #433 Pat Dalton	$2.50
___ 0-425-10682-9	SURRENDER THE DAWN #434 Jan Mathews	$2.50
___ 0-425-10683-7	A WARM DECEMBER #435 Jacqueline Topaz	$2.50
___ 0-425-10708-6	RAINBOW'S END #436 Carole Buck (On sale Apr. '88)	$2.50
___ 0-425-10709-4	TEMPTRESS #437 Linda Raye (On sale Apr. '88)	$2.50

Please send the titles I've checked above. Mail orders to:

BERKLEY PUBLISHING GROUP
390 Murray Hill Pkwy., Dept. B
East Rutherford, NJ 07073

POSTAGE & HANDLING:
$1.00 for one book, $.25 for each
additional. Do not exceed $3.50.

NAME _____

ADDRESS _____

CITY _____

STATE _____ ZIP _____

Please allow 6 weeks for delivery.
Prices are subject to change without notice.

BOOK TOTAL	$_____
SHIPPING & HANDLING	$_____
APPLICABLE SALES TAX (CA, NJ, NY, PA)	$_____
TOTAL AMOUNT DUE PAYABLE IN US FUNDS. (No cash orders accepted.)	$_____

NORMA BEISHIR'S
"DANCE OF THE GODS

Has got it all! **Mystery and megabucks, thrills and chills, sex and romance. This is a runaway rollercoaster ride which grips you from page one and races to its explosive climax!"**

—Judith Gould,
Bestselling author of *SINS*

Players in Paradise...
from the ultra-exclusive reaches of Malibu and Beverly Hills, to the glittering playgrounds of New York and Paris, Meredith and Alexander's passion was a fantasy come true. Their fame and fortune granted them everything in the world. But nothing could hush the sizzling secret that would link Alexander to a hidden past, and lead them both through the ultimate scandal...

—— **DANCE OF THE GODS** Norma Beishir
0-425-10839-2/$4.50 On sale in May '88

Please send the titles I've checked above. Mail orders to:

BERKLEY PUBLISHING GROUP
390 Murray Hill Pkwy., Dept. B
East Rutherford, NJ 07073

NAME _____

ADDRESS _____

CITY _____

STATE _____ ZIP _____

Please allow 6 weeks for delivery.
Prices are subject to change without notice.

POSTAGE & HANDLING:
$1.00 for one book, $.25 for each
additional. Do not exceed $3.50.

BOOK TOTAL $_____

SHIPPING & HANDLING $_____

APPLICABLE SALES TAX $_____
(CA, NJ, NY, PA)

TOTAL AMOUNT DUE $_____
PAYABLE IN US FUNDS.
(No cash orders accepted.)